2

ROSEMARY'S GLOVE

Other books by Shirley Raye Redmond:

Stone of the Sun

ROSEMARY'S GLOVE

•

Shirley Raye Redmond

AVALON BOOKS
NEW YORK

Library of Congress Cataloging-in-Publication Data

Redmond, Shirley-Raye, 1955-
    Rosemary's glove / Shirley Raye Redmond.
        p.   cm.
    ISBN 978-0-8034-9957-7
    1. Young women—England—Fiction.   2. Aristocracy
(Social class)—Fiction.   3. Mate selection—Fiction.   I. Title.

    PS3568.E364R67   2009
    813'.54—dc22
                                                          2008052528

PRINTED IN THE UNITED STATES OF AMERICA
ON ACID-FREE PAPER
BY HADDON CRAFTSMEN, BLOOMSBURG, PENNSYLVANIA

For Susan Kestell, Kelly Hakonson and Jennifer McKerley with love and gratitude.

Chapter One

"Come, sit down beside me, my dear. I wish to speak with you," Mrs. Addison said. Had the widow not been so agitated, she would have noticed the dark shadows under her daughter's eyes and Rosemary's strangely subdued manner. But, as Gladys Addison was consumed by matters of self-consideration, she did *not* notice. She merely patted the sofa invitingly, and glanced up at Rosemary with a slight smile.

"We must have a little chat," Mrs. Addison said. "I have something of great importance to share with you."

"Yes, Mama." Rosemary seated herself submissively on the sofa. Despite her own troubles, the young lady— nearer the age of twenty than not—observed the rapid blinking of Mrs. Addison's eyes and realized, with wariness, that her mother was disturbed about something.

1

Whenever the widow was over-anxious or upset by one thing or another, her eyes blinked excessively. Rosemary braced herself for a scold. "As you have no doubt noticed, Rosemary, Mr. Nevin has been all that is kind, so very attentive," her mother began hesitantly. "His lineage is impeccable, his manner is quite . . . er . . . faultless." The widow paused, noting the candid interest on her daughter's beautiful face. Blinking several times in rapid succession, she blurted out, "Mr. Nevin has asked me to be his wife, and I have accepted him!"

If Rosemary was disconcerted by the fact that her mother had received an offer of marriage in the middle of the London season before she herself had contracted an eligible connection, her demeanor did not show it. Her slender white hands rested quietly in her lap. Mrs. Addison noted that her daughter's blue eyes, fringed by long, thick lashes, shone with warmth and good humor. Her lovely young face—with its pert nose, full lips, and a beauty mark upon the left cheek—was framed by a glorious cluster of honey-colored curls.

"Oh, Mama, how famous!" Rosemary declared in all sincerity, reaching out both hands to squeeze her mother's between her own. Although he was not handsome or rich or even charming, Mr. Edgar Nevin *was* a gentleman of good character and a comfortable income. Despite his impatient manner and his tendency to rush about as though in frantic turmoil, he *was* kind in a rather brusque way. Rosemary had observed that the gentleman was obviously quite smitten by her quiet, gentle mother.

"I guessed you were not indifferent to him," Rosemary added, touched by the rising color in her mother's pale cheeks. "I *do* wish you all the happiness in the world, Mama!"

"Thank you, my dear." She was much gratified by her dear girl's solicitations. "You must realize, however, that we are not announcing our engagement until after *you* have accepted a suitable offer of marriage." She paused, regarding Rosemary's smiling face with a pinched expression about her mouth. Her eyes blinked with fierce anxiety.

"You see," she went on awkwardly, "it's not *seemly* that I should marry again before . . . er . . . before I have made a match for you, and that's the problem I wish to speak to you about."

Rosemary raised a delicate eyebrow. Her lips twitched with some secret amusement. "What? Have you despaired *already* of marrying me off to an eligible suitor? I should not fret if I were you. The problem lies not in *finding* a suitable husband but in selecting *only* one, which I believe is all that I'm allowed under the law."

If Rosemary was just a little vain it was understandable. Ever since the girl had been introduced into Society the year before, she had been hailed as The Beauty, The Incomparable, The Nonpareil. Offers of marriage had been showered upon her with such intensity that the awed Mrs. Addison had, in a private conversation with her mother-in-law, likened it to a hailstorm.

Now, although nearly twenty and in the midst of her second season, Rosemary Addison was even more sought after. The polished sophistication she had acquired the year before had added considerably to her charms. And if her beauty and good nature did not recommend her as a marriageable prize, then her fortune certainly did. It was a well known and frequently pointed out fact that the chit was indecently wealthy!

"You've not yet given up hope, I pray," Rosemary teased. "Surely, you are not ready to retire me to the shelf!"

"Of course not!" her mother declared heatedly. "All of London know you're a matrimonial prize! And I'm well aware of the number of offers you have received—*and* refused. You can afford to be particular," Mrs. Addison pointed out proudly. "I also quite understand your desire to marry a man of your own choosing, one for whom you feel . . . er . . . some affection." Here, Mrs. Addison paused again. "However, there isn't much time . . . for you to settle upon the gentleman of your choice."

"Not much time?" Rosemary asked, tipping her head to one side. For the moment, she decided it would be best to shove her own gloomy problems to the back of her mind and to attend closely to her aggrieved mother. "What do you mean, Mama?" she asked with a puzzled frown.

"Well, as you know, Mr. Nevin is connected with the Foreign Office." Mrs. Addison gave several forceful blinks. "He's to journey to India this autumn, and he wishes me to accompany him—as his wife." She pulled a handkerchief from the small, concealed pocket of her lavender morning dress. She glanced up briefly to note Rosemary's reaction to this unexpected news.

But her daughter, again, seemed delighted. "How exciting! Such an adventure for you, Mama!"

"Yes, my dear, certainly. But you do not seem to *fully understand* the situation." Looking down at the handkerchief in her trembling hands, the nervous matron began to fold it methodically. "You see, I cannot *possibly* marry Edgar—dear Mr. Nevin—until *you* are wed. He suggests that you accept one of your suitor's offers as soon as possible, so that I can make the marriage arrangements and see you satisfactorily established before we—Mr. Nevin and I—leave for India at the end of October."

Mrs. Addison looked up from the mutilation of her handkerchief. She gazed hopefully into her daughter's beautiful but puzzled face.

"Why is it necessary that I marry before you journey to India with Mr. Nevin?"

This innocent inquiry caused her nervous mother to gasp. Rosemary hastened to continue. "I could remain here with my grandmother and enjoy another season, if I so choose. I don't see why *my* marital status, or lack thereof, need interfere with *your* plans at all!"

"Why, it would be scandalous, Rosemary! What would people think? It simply wouldn't be condoned!" Mrs. Addison's anxious face diffused with color. "I could never shirk my God-given responsibility, simply to satisfy my . . . my own fervent, heartfelt wishes!"

"I see," Rosemary replied, frowning.

Mrs. Addison's face took on a hopeful glow. "Do you, my dear? Edgar—I mean, Mr. Nevin—said you would. For if I do not accompany him on this voyage, it will be years—*three long years*—before he returns to England."

At this point, Mrs. Addison, though still blinking profusely, blushed like a schoolroom miss. "Dear Mr. Nevin said that once I impressed upon you how desirous we both are of going out to India together—as man and wife—he was certain that you would not wish to stand in the way of our happiness."

"No, Mama, I would not wish to do so," Rosemary admitted feelingly. She was well aware of how lonely her mother had been ever since George Addison, Rosemary's handsome, good-natured father, had succumbed to pneumonia five years ago. In truth, the heiress was more than happy that her shy, gentle mother had formed an attachment with a suitable gentleman.

"Edgar—dear Mr. Nevin—has pointed out, and rightly so, that this isn't your *first* Season—you had a grand come-out last year. He said we should not feel at all hesitant in expecting you to select a suitable offer at the end of *this* season."

"And what else has your dear Mr. Nevin said?" Rosemary asked dryly. She could feel her cheeks growing pink with displeasure.

"He mentioned that as you've had *so many* offers, that it would be extremely selfish on your part not to accept one of the gentlemen as soon as possible." Her mother was in a breathless rush. "So, you see, you *must* decide which offer meets with your approval, accept the fortunate gentleman, and then I can place an order for your wedding gown, and begin packing for my journey to India. With your cooperation, everything will work out splendidly. I will give you until the end of the Season to make up your mind."

Having concluded the discussion, which she had been dreading, Gladys Addison sank back against the sofa cushions with a notable sigh of relief. Rosemary, on the other hand, simmering with anger, sat rigidly still. Her countenance, though seemingly unmoved, was like the calm before a storm. Outwardly, she was quiet and self–controlled; inwardly, she raged! How dare Mr. Nevin—that impatient bagpipe—rush *her* into a marriage for *his* convenience! How dare her mother allow it?

"And if I do *not* choose to marry at the end of the Season, what then?" Rosemary's eyes glinted dangerously.

Mrs. Addison immediately sat forward, a stern frown on her face. It was obvious that she found the very possibility unpalatable. "Why, then Mr. Nevin will have to journey to India without me. It may be years before we see one another again, Rosemary. Surely, you would not be so thoughtless?"

Her mother's references to thoughtlessness brought Rosemary's own problems rushing painfully back to the forefront of her tormented mind. The image of Lord Beverley's devilishly handsome countenance pained her even further. With his curly black hair, his piercing blue eyes, his sensuous mouth and glib conversation, the earl was London's most attractive rake. He was also impoverished—everyone in London knew it—and if he was determined to marry an heiress in order to maintain his present lifestyle, it was certainly understandable.

What *wasn't* understandable to Rosemary, or to the puzzled beau monde, was why the dashing earl had not yet offered for the Season's most desirable heiress. How dare the conceited rogue not offer for her! Every other fortune hunter had taken pains to, Rosemary reflected. For a brief moment, she allowed herself to contemplate the pleasing image of the earl's handsome face, his broad shoulders, his feline grace in the ballroom. Money trickled through his fingers like water some said, and everyone knew that his lordship must marry money *and soon.* Why had he not already, Rosemary wondered in silent agony?

When she had made her debut into Society the previous Season, Rosemary had enchanted the earl with her exquisite beauty and fresh charm. She'd heard whispered rumors that bets had been placed at one of London's more prestigious gentlemen's clubs that Beverley—the dashing wastrel—would wed Miss Addison before the Season's end. When the expected match was *not* made, Society raised its collective eyebrows in astonishment.

Perhaps no one was more surprised than Rosemary herself. She well knew that Lord Beverley was not indifferent to her. For her part, she was quite captivated by his handsome countenance and gallant address. He was more than charming—he was everything she wanted in a husband. Because he was so very attractive and had a title, Rosemary was more than willing to accept his offer of marriage. She realized that Beverley was proud and that offering for her because his pockets were let would, to some minor degree, disturb his dignity. And so, she'd made up her mind to cultivate patience, a virtue she did not possess in any admirable quantity. She waited for nearly a year for the earl to come up to scratch. But he had not. When Rosemary didn't make a brilliant match at the end of her first Season, despite everyone's expectations, she merely smiled. Now, in the middle of her second Season, Rosemary was still receiving offers of marriage at a fairly brisk rate and refusing them with equal dispatch. Her heart was set stubbornly upon Lord Beverley—but her patience was running thin.

"Oh, Rosemary, you will consider your mother's happiness as well as your own, won't you, my dear?"

Rosemary, roused from her reverie, nodded her honeygold head. How could she tell her concerned mother that the only man she intended to marry had not yet made an offer? *Nor will he until he's had his sport,* Rosemary thought bitterly. How dare the man keep her dangling while he clung so tenaciously to his impoverished bachelorhood!

Her eyes narrowed and took on a rather smoky hue as she recalled a conversation, which she had accidentally overheard recently at the Bancrofts' ball. At the time, Rosemary had excused herself from her throng of ardent admirers to see to the repair of a torn flounce. Hot, flushed, and desirous of a moment of solitary fresh air, she had quietly stepped out onto the portico, pleased to have escaped unnoticed by her fervent beaus. Two men were blowing a cloud in the garden beyond. They did not hear nor see Rosemary's approach, as she was concealed from view by a large oleander. Neither did Rosemary actually see the gentlemen. She only saw the smoke and heard their voices.

"If you don't come up to scratch soon, Tom old boy, somebody else is going to cut you out."

Rosemary had immediately recognized Sir Alfred Falkner's familiar drawl. Listening more closely, she'd heard him say, "The chit won't wait forever. She's every bit as proud as you are. If you put her nose out of joint, she'll accept another's offer."

Then she heard the other man chuckle, and her pulse raced when he spoke. "Have no fears, Freddie. The Incomparable will have none other. I've seen that adoring glint in her lovely blue eyes when she looks upon me—

and more than once. I dare say her mother wants to get her hands on my title as much as I want to get my hands on the Addison fortune."

"Well, Lord Darlington has offered for her, I know," Falkner went on, a note of concern in his voice. "And rumor has it that Chesford will try *his* luck as well, if he hasn't already done so. The girl can have her pick of titles, if *that's* what she's after."

"Freddie, I assure you that Miss Addison is mine for the asking," Lord Beverley had replied smugly.

Rosemary had not waited to hear any more. With her cheeks burning and her heart pounding, she had fled from the portico to seek solitary solace in one of the Bancrofts' empty sitting rooms. It took considerable effort to staunch the flow of hot, angry tears that spilled down her flushed cheeks. How could Beverley be so cruel? Hadn't she allowed him an entire Season to work up the nerve to ask her to marry? Had she not suffered the chagrin of remaining unmarried while homelier girls with smaller fortunes had made acceptable matches? She was certain he intended to ask for her hand in marriage—eventually. He had been an attentive suitor, singling her out at every ball and party, even sending flowers with romantic poems attached.

"Well, my lord, you leave me no choice but to force your hand!" Rosemary had murmured angrily between clenched teeth. Title indeed! Why, the Duke of Rothersham had shown considerable interest in her himself. With little effort on her part, Rosemary *could be* a duchess, *if* she *wanted* to marry Rothersham, who was plagued with gout and old enough to be her grandfather! It was intolerable that Lord Beverley should toy with her affections so lightly. With fierce resolve, Rosemary vowed that night to give the handsome earl his comeuppance.

She had returned to the ballroom after regaining her composure. Seeking out her mother, Rosemary quietly confided that she had a headache and begged to return home at once. Mrs. Addison, glancing at her daughter's flushed face and bright eyes, became concerned that the girl was taking a fever, and immediately called for the carriage and made their excuses to their hostess. Once at home, Rosemary allowed her maid to undress her, submitted to her mother's tender ministrations and then tumbled wearily into bed.

She did not sleep, however, but had stared at the ceiling hoping some plan would miraculously unfold itself there for her perusal. An idea had indeed taken shape in her fevered brain but sleep had remained elusive. Thus Rosemary appeared now before her mother with purplish shadows beneath her eyes—a circumstance that Mrs. Addison had failed to observe because of her own unrelieved anxieties.

"What about Lord Beverley?" Mrs. Addison was saying.

"What about him?" Rosemary asked, sitting up a bit straighter and forcing herself to attend to her mother's inquiries.

"I have wondered . . . if perhaps, you might . . . have a special interest in his lordship?"

"Not particularly," Rosemary lied. "But I believe he has a particular interest in me." She held her hands tightly in her lap, hoping their slight tremor would not reveal her own agitation. Her mother sighed. "He has been so very attentive. I had hoped . . ." Mrs. Addison paused. "It would be a fine thing to be a countess, my dear," she added, with an unsteady smile.

Rosemary thought so too. Placing a hand to her eyes, she asked to be excused. "I still suffer with the headache, Mama, and would beg your leave to return to my room."

"Certainly, my dear!" Mrs. Addison stood and touched Rosemary's shoulder lightly. "Now that you bring it to my attention, I see that you do not look at all well. Bathe your head with violet water, my dear." She leaned over then and kissed her daughter softly on the cheek.

"You are a good girl, Rosemary. I'm quite pleased with you. I know that I can trust you to make a suitable, if not a brilliant match, by the end of the Season. My happiness rests in your hands and I know you will not take this responsibility lightly."

Dismissed with these weighty words, Rosemary did not return to her room but sought out her grandmother instead. She found that worthy woman in the library, as usual, working on her novel-in-progress. Emily Addison, a spry, silver-haired widow much taken with Fanny Burney's prose, had decided to write a novel of her own.

"Gran-Gran, may I have a word with you?" Rosemary

interrupted, using the childish name she had fondly given her favorite grandparent in her nursery days.

"Certainly!" Emily declared with an affectionate smile for the granddaughter who had taken after her in beauty as well as vitality. Despite her advanced age, the silver hair and the tell-tale lines upon her face, Emily Addison was attractive still. She folded her long, slender, ink-stained hands upon the desk.

"You look burnt to the socket, Rosie!"

Rosemary lowered herself into the chair beside her grandmother's cluttered desk. She licked her dry lips and mustered up her courage. The success of her plan to win Lord Beverley's love rested, in no small part, upon her grandmother's unknowing assistance.

"I find myself in need of a repairing lease, Gran. I would like to retire to Oakley for a few weeks. I wonder if you would accompany me?"

"What? In the middle of the Season?" The woman watched Rosemary's face with sharp eyes as blue as the heiress' own.

"Yes, ma'am," Rosemary replied meekly. "I'm not feeling at all the thing these days."

"Have you consulted your mother about the matter?"

"No, I had hoped you would bring it up to her in my stead. She'll be quite scandalized, I suppose. But she'll soon recover. Mr. Nevin has asked Mama to marry him and she has accepted. She would dislike leaving town at the moment, I think."

Her grandmother's eyebrows shot up in mild surprise. "Gladys remarrying? This is news indeed!"

"Besides," Rosemary said, reaching for her grandmother's inky fingers and giving them an affectionate squeeze, "I would much rather have *your* company at Oakley, and you will get more writing done. There will be fewer interruptions."

"Well, I should hope so!" Emily Addison declared emphatically. "Between the hordes of suitors that overrun this house longing for a glimpse of you, and the gaggle of gossips that come to visit your mother, I scarcely have a quiet moment to myself!"

Rosemary giggled. Her grandmother cocked her head to one side and regarded the girl before her with a keen eye. "You're not running away from anything, are you, Rosemary? I will not condone cowardice."

"No, Gran, I am not running away." Rosemary's chin thrust itself upward. She regarded her grandmother with frankness. "You see, Mama wants me to marry at the end of the Season, so that *she* can marry dear Mr. Nevin and journey with him to India come autumn."

"You don't say!" Her grandmother's eyes glistened with amused interest.

Rosemary nodded. Then turning, she noticed a single, lavender glove upon the marble-topped table across the room. Using this as an excuse to escape her grandmother's scrutiny, Rosemary walked toward the table to claim the mislaid item. "I need to do some serious reflection," she said, forcing a sigh. Softly, she counted to twenty and then turned around to face her grandmother.

"Will two weeks be sufficient?" the elder Mrs. Addison asked, regarding Rosemary tenderly.

"Two weeks should be adequate, I think. No more than three, surely." If she played her cards right, three weeks would be more than sufficient, Rosemary knew.

"All right then, I shall fix things up with your mother," Emily declared, noting the becoming flush which heightened her granddaughter's complexion. "I don't know what you're up to, you clever minx, and I don't want to know—for fear I'll disapprove. But I'll go to Oakley with you since you wish it."

"Gran!" Rosemary protested with an astonished glint in her wide, innocent eyes. "I'm not up to anything, as you put it. *Truly!*"

"Fiddlesticks!" her discerning grandmother declared.

Chapter Two

With the competent authority born of wealth and superior social rank, Emily Addison made all the necessary arrangements for journeying to Oakley with immediate dispatch. She also squelched her daughter-in-law's protests.

"The child is nearly done in—anyone can see that!" Emily told her. "Rosemary needs to recuperate her strength and her spirits. No one will want to marry her if she goes about looking like a pudding face."

"But in the midst of the Season!" Gladys wailed.

"It can't be helped," Emily replied, unmoved by her daughter-in-law's distress. "But her ardent beaus will renew their suits with increased vigor once Rosie returns to town. A clever stratagem, don't you agree?"

Gladys Addison did *not* agree, but was unable to

admit it to her authoritative mother-in-law. It was with a great deal of reluctance that she saw her daughter off in the carriage, and with more reluctance still, she acquiesced to Emily's demand that she not give Rosemary's direction to every gentleman who requested it.

"We don't want any moon-faced beaus presenting themselves on our doorstep at Oakley Manor," the dowager declared with a dismissive wave of her blue-veined hand. "Rosemary won't be able to recover herself if she is forced to endure Mr. Parker's insipid verse or Lord Darlington's painfully stammered declarations of love."

So, despite her mother's objections, Rosemary posted down to Oakley for a short period of rustication, with only her obliging grandmother in attendance. Their dressers, not needed, were given a holiday. Gladys Addison was left behind to console the heiress' dismayed suitors and to make the girl's apologies to astonished hostesses.

However, when Lord Beverley called the very afternoon following Rosemary's departure, Mrs. Addison found him more difficult to appease. Truth to tell, the woman was thrilled by the earl's polite but persistent inquiries about her absent daughter, and she clung to the hope that an offer of marriage would not be too far off on the romantic horizon.

"Truly, my lord, there's no need to concern yourself on Rosemary's behalf," Mrs. Addison said with a tremulous smile. Really, the man was too attractive for his own good, she thought, noting the crisp dark curls and the penetrating blue eyes. What a fine-looking couple he and Rosemary would make!

"My daughter has been suffering with megrims of late, and her appetite has been poor," she stammered. "The physician prescribed a brief respite from social obligations and has sent Rosemary into the country for some fresh air and plain food—only for a week or two. I'm certain that once she returns, Rosemary will be delighted to go riding with you in the park."

"I will look forward to the day, madam," his lordship said with one of his easy smiles. "Perhaps in the meantime, if you would consent to it, I could send Miss Addison a brief missive expressing my eagerness for her return. May I have her address?"

Recalling her mother-in-law's strict admonition, Gladys stammered. "I have paper and ink here in the parlor, should you care to write a few lines now. I will see that Rosemary gets your letter."

Beverley hastily scribbled his best wishes to the absent heiress, and again gently pressed Mrs. Addison for Rosemary's direction. She remained steadfast and would not reveal it. His lordship was forced to take his leave without the information he desired.

But Beverley was not to be fobbed off so easily, nor was he convinced that the beautiful heiress was away under the order of a physician. At the Bancrofts' ball, Rosemary had been in high bloom, he recalled suspiciously. Having pressed Mrs. Addison for Rosemary's whereabouts and having been so adroitly refused, the earl's suspicious nature was more than a little piqued. He made it his business, or rather that of his most trusted footman, to make discreet inquiries among Mrs. Addison's staff.

Learning that Rosemary had left London for Oakley in the company of her fraternal grandmother, Lord Beverley smiled, reassured. The girl must indeed be on a repairing lease, for Oakley was a secluded country manor where Rosemary would find but a mere handful of country squires to dazzle with her impaired beauty. There was certainly no need for his lordship to concern himself with such paltry competition. Beverley silently wished the young heiress well, for *surely* she must be burnt to the socket to risk leaving London in the midst of the Season.

Meanwhile, Emily Addison, on her way to that secluded country manor in her well-sprung carriage, with Rosemary seated across from her, was convinced that her granddaughter was most certainly hatching a plot. But what kind of scheme Emily could not say.

The girl is in no more need of recuperation than I am, she thought as she observed Rosemary's complexion and sparkling eyes. Indeed, Rosemary seemed to glow with vitality. And when Mr. Gordon Stanley-Hodge, the Addisons' eccentric country neighbor and long-time family friend, hearing of the ladies' arrival, sent over an invitation for them to join him for dinner, Emily noted that Rosemary positively bloomed with anticipation. The girl prepared for the simple country dinner as though they were attending one of London's more infamous squeezes. When she came downstairs in a gown of pale, lemon-colored crape over a slip of white sarsnet, Emily raised an elegant eyebrow in mild surprise and wisely chose to say nothing.

Curiosity of another sort, however, got the best of her. "What, pray tell, is this?" Emily inquired, after she and Rosemary climbed into the carriage on their way to dinner at Hodge Hall. She had watched with some apprehension as Chumley supervised the careful installation of a cumbersome wooden crate into the carriage at the ladies' feet. This same box had come all the way down from London with them, and as Rosemary seemed especially concerned about its welfare, it piqued her grandmother's curiosity.

"Why, it's a birthday present for Broderick," Rosemary declared, thanking Chumley for his assistance and taking a small, white box tied with golden cord from his gloved hands. "And this is for Uncle Gordon," she added.

"Is he having a birthday too?" Emily inquired lazily, recognizing the box which, she had little doubt, contained some delectable confection from Gunter's.

"No, it's just a little token of my esteem," Rosemary said, with a beguiling smile.

"And will you not tell me what *that* box contains?" Emily asked, her eyes narrowing as they studied the mysterious crate.

"You must wait and see!" Rosemary declared in a

teasing manner. "I only hope Broderick doesn't already have one—one of this particular quality, at least."

"Is it something expensive then?"

"Oh, very!" Rosemary replied with a twinkle in her eyes.

"Well, then, surely Broderick doesn't own one—he's a pauper! Hasn't a groat to his name." Her grandmother slumped against the carriage cushions as the driver took a corner.

"That's not true! Uncle Gordon has bought him an annuity. And as he lives so very frugally, Broderick may well have been able to afford to purchase such an item for himself. It's just the kind of thing he *would* buy—rather than horses or clothes. I hope Uncle Gordon didn't buy one for him already." A frown creased her brow.

"Oh, you can be sure they've not had the time to buy presents for one another—with all the gallivanting they've been doing," Emily said with a note of disapproval in her tone. "America! Umph! That's a long way to go for a few beetles, I must say!"

Rosemary chuckled. "Beetles *and* plants, Gran. Don't forget that Broderick collects flowers. He's a botanist."

Emily gave a genteel snort. "Botanist! Bugs! They are both off their heads! Gordon has simply ruined the boy. One's just as eccentric as the other. A fine guardian Gordon has proven to be, that's all I can say! Broderick's dear mother would not have approved. She was a very quiet, well-bred creature, and quite attractive, as I recall. Of course, her husband, Charles Loren, was just as much of an oddball as Gordon."

The elder Mrs. Addison then launched into a familiar tirade against Mr. Gordon Stanley-Hodge, as well as his former ward, Broderick Loren, who had willingly turned their backs upon society to pursue scientific studies.

"When one is as rich as Uncle Gordon, one can do as one pleases."

Although Mr. Stanley-Hodge was not, in fact, her uncle or a relative of any sort, Rosemary had developed a lasting friendship with the elderly bachelor from the time, when only four years old, she had presented him with a squashed beetle for his collection. That eccentric gentleman had been enchanted by the little girl's childish charms and impressed with her pluck. He had likened her lovely coloring to that of a pink-tinged yellow rose and had promptly dubbed her his "little Rosebud," a name by which he'd fondly called her ever since.

"Wealth does not grant one a license for abnormality," Emily went on.

"Broderick and Uncle Gordon are not abnormal! They are simply . . . umm . . ."—she tried to find a suitable term to describe the two men of whom she'd grown particularly fond over the years—"they are *colorful!*"

"Colorful, indeed!" her grandmother responded with

emotion. "I still say, it's unnatural for grown men to spend their time sticking pins into bugs and traipsing about the world in search of flower petals to press between the pages of an album! It's unnatural!"

If the personalities of the two gentlemen in question were considered abnormal, Mrs. Addison could find no fault with their appearances as they strode out to greet the ladies upon their arrival at Hodge Hall. Gordon Stanley-Hodge was a very tall man built upon long, lean angular lines. Even at four-and-sixty, he was unstooped by age or infirmity. His face, framed by a cloud of snow-white hair, was red and heavily lined from years of exposure to the sun. His large nose was hawkish. His pale grey eyes were good–humored and glittered now with unconcealed delight at beholding Rosemary again.

Mr. Broderick Loren looked remarkably well in a coat of olive-green superfine, gleaming boots and a modest neck cloth. His long legs were sheathed in tight pantaloons and his serious countenance was handsomely transformed by a broad smile. Mrs. Addison silently concluded that gallivanting around the globe had not taken its toll upon her neighbors' appearances, at least.

"Uncle Gordon! How wonderful to see you again!" Rosemary exclaimed as that gentleman assisted his young guest from the carriage. They embraced fondly.

"Rosebud! Look at you! A beauty and no mistake!" Mr. Stanley-Hodge declared, pleased by the girl's affectionate greeting.

Rosemary beamed upon him and then turned to clutch

the hands of his younger companion. "Ricky, how well you look! And I'm certain you're even taller than before."

Mr. Loren, delighted by her use of his childhood nickname, shook his head with admiration. "It's been an age, Rosie," he greeted her with an easy, familiar grace. "How elegant you've become."

"And you're as dark as a gypsy, I declare!" Emily said, noting the young man's skin, bronzed from exposure to the elements.

"Gypsy, indeed!" Mr. Loren replied with mock objection. "You offend my scholarly sensibilities, Mrs. Addison." He grinned then, and Emily observed once again how satisfactorily young Broderick's face was transformed when he smiled, revealing strong, white teeth, and a warm twinkle in his light brown eyes. Despite Gordon's dubious influence, Emily decided that his ward had not turned out so badly after all.

Rosemary squeezed Broderick's hands more tightly between her own and then followed him gaily into the house, asking the butler to see to the boxes in the carriage. Mr. Stanley-Hodge offered his arm to Mrs. Addison.

"I declare the gel is a beauty! She must surely take the shine out of all the other females in London," he said with a touch of pride. "No missish airs, either. No schoolroom insipidity!"

"I declare, Rosie, every eligible man in town shall have offered for you by now!" Broderick threw in gallantly, having overheard the older man's comment.

He looked down into Rosemary's smiling, upturned face. If his heart jolted at what he saw there, he put it down to astonishment that the skinny, colt-legged little girl with whom he used to play had been transformed into so devastating a creature.

"Not quite all the gentlemen," Rosemary replied, lowering her lashes and thinking briefly of the charming but elusive Lord Beverley.

"What brings you to Oakley?" Mr. Stanley-Hodge demanded. "I'm not such a rustic that I don't know it's the middle of the London Season!" he declared with some feeling.

"We are escaping the smothering cluster of lovesick swains," Emily Addison told him, as she seated herself in the stiff-backed chair he indicated in the drawing room. "We live in constant fear that my daughter-in-law's house will collapse beneath the onslaught. A body can't think straight with all the comings and goings! And the aroma of the bouquets and nosegays that arrive all day long is quite cloying."

Despite her complaints, Emily's tone was noticeably tinged with pride. Her granddaughter was a great success! And no one was more pleased by Rosemary's popularity than her grandmother. Emily had never had a daughter of her own to bring out, and she counted herself fortunate to share, even in a small way, Rosemary's introduction into society.

Rosemary blushed and quickly changed the subject. "I want to hear all about your voyage to America," she demanded. "Your letters were most intriguing," she addressed Broderick. "Now tell us all that you left out."

But before Mr. Loren could comply, dinner was announced and the party removed to the dining room, where the four enjoyed a leisurely meal of lobster, chicken, and pickled salmon, accompanied by fresh vegetables and fruits—many of which had come to the table straight from Mr. Loren's notable greenhouse.

"Not much of a dinner party," Mr. Stanley-Hodge apologized. "I had thought of inviting the vicar and his daughter, but Miss Thatcher bestows such *poignant* glances at poor Broderick that it throws him quite out of countenance." He noted the young man's flushed cheeks and cast a twisted smile in Rosemary's direction. "So, I thought, we'd better make do with just ourselves. More comfortable for all concerned."

Rosemary noted Broderick's embarrassment with quiet amusement. She quickly took a bite of a parslied new potato in an attempt to suppress a rising giggle. The very idea of her sober young friend arousing the romantic interests of a young lady was truly laughable. Everyone knew that Broderick Loren was dedicated to scholarship. He had no time for, nor interest in, romantic pursuits.

"Now, about America!" Rosemary demanded, coming nobly to Broderick's rescue.

"Shall I begin with our American adventures or start with an anecdote about our stay in the Bahamas?" Mr. Loren asked, rewarding Rosemary with a grateful smile.

"The Bahamas!" Emily declared, shaking her silver head in disbelief. "It is no wonder we've not seen you for two years! So, you journeyed to the islands as well?" "Indeed, we did!" Mr. Stanley-Hodge replied. "We've only made it back to Hodge Hall in the past fortnight. And already, I miss the Caribbean. Why, it was a beetle collector's paradise," he told her with enthusiasm, and proceeded to regale his guests with lively accounts of their adventures abroad.

"America is a beautiful country and a vast one," Broderick told them, picking up the tale after Gordon paused to refresh himself with wine. "We spent most of our time taking long walks in search of new specimens for our respective collections. In fact," he added, a glint of humor lighting his soft, brown eyes, "we earned the nicknames of Mr. Bugs and Mr. Blooms."

Rosemary laughed delightedly, and her grandmother, again noting the young man's becoming yet boyish grin, interjected, "So you did cultivate a few acquaintances? You didn't spend *all* of your time roaming about the countryside?"

"We mingled with plenty of people," Gordon told her. "The Americans are quite friendly, considering." He paused briefly, wondered about launching into a discussion of the political situation in the New World, and then decided against it. "We met many interesting individuals."

"And what of your specimens?" Rosemary wanted

to know, reaching for her water goblet. "Did you bring many back with you?

Uncle Gordon snorted. "Orchids, giant ferns, not to mention banana plants! *Where* Rick is going to put them all, I can't imagine. That greenhouse of his is nearly bursting at the seams. Poor Tupp will be run off his legs trying to help this young jackanapes get everything in order!"

"And what about your precious beetles, Uncle Gordon?" Rosemary teased. "No doubt you'll be quite busy yourself pinning the poor creatures into their frames and cataloguing your new additions."

"Oh, he brought back butterflies as well as beetles," Broderick spoke up. "He's starting a *new* collection!"

The dinner concluded as gaily as it had begun, and when the women excused themselves and made their way to the drawing room, Mr. Loren and Mr. Stanley-Hodge hastily partook of their after-dinner port and joined them almost immediately. Rosemary clasped one of Broderick's hands as he passed by her chair, and she smiled up into his serious young face with an eager twinkle in her eyes.

"I've brought a present for you, Ricky—a belated birthday present. I want you to open it right away—it's over there." She indicated the mysterious wooden crate that had intrigued her grandmother.

"And this one's for you, Uncle Gordon," the heiress said gaily, handing over the white box tied with golden cord.

"It's not *my* birthday!" the elderly gentlemen declared in a gruff manner, which belied the pleasure he in fact felt at the girl's thoughtfulness.

"Oh, I know that! This is merely a small homecoming present. Just a little something for your sweet tooth!"

"Open it, Broderick!" Emily Addison insisted, turning her attention to the young man who was studying the crate with some perplexity. "Rosemary has kept me in suspense these past few days, and I'm eager to see what surprise that crate contains. Do open it."

"Yes, open it!" Gordon urged, "before you turn yet another year older, while we sit here waiting for you to do so!"

"How old in fact are you?" Emily asked.

"I recently turned seven-and-twenty," Broderick replied absently, his attention consumed by the crate's contents.

"What?" Rosemary declared in feigned surprise. "So old as that?"

Broderick grinned at her, but Gordon snorted contemptuously.

"Old?" he shouted heatedly. "Bah! Broderick's a mere puppy! Old, indeed! I daresay, Rosebud, you must think *I* am ready to stick my spoon in the wall any time now!"

Rosemary's gurgling laughter filled the room. "*Dear Uncle Gordon! I was only teasing.*" Gordon, his eyes as merry as her own, nodded in a mollified way.

Turning then to Broderick, Rosemary said in a more serious tone, "I do hope it isn't damaged. Shumway, my mother's man of business, assured me that it had been packed most carefully."

Noting the queer expression on Broderick's face as he gazed into the opened crate, Gordon and Emily abandoned their chairs and moved towards the young gentleman for a better view of that which held his rapt attention.

"Oh, Rosie, you shouldn't have!" Broderick declared, plunging his hands into the straw-filled crate. He gently pulled out a strange-looking contraption that seemed to fill him with considerable awe. A trembling smile curled Rosemary's lips ever so slightly.

"What, pray tell, is it?" Emily asked, unimpressed.

"Why, it's a new microscope!" Gordon declared as he stepped forward for a better view. "And the latest model too!"

"Do you like it, Rick?" Rosemary's eyes watched her friend's stern face softened by obvious pleasure. "You don't, I hope, already have one like it?"

"No, no, I do not," he murmured, his attention still entirely consumed by his unexpected gift. "We're still using an old modified Van Leeuwenhoek model. This is quite beyond words." His face glowed with undisguised pleasure. "Gordon, come look at these lenses."

Then turning to Rosemary, he declared, "Rosie, you shouldn't have! It's too dear!"

"I should say it *is* dear!" Gordon agreed. One knowing glance at the treasured article, and that eccentric gentleman was well aware of the expense involved. "Must have put you back a pretty guinea or two! What made you throw your money away on such a fiddlehead?"

"Ricky's not a fiddlehead, and well you know it! He's a scholar, and one day he'll make quite a name for himself, I've no doubt of it. And besides, I missed his two previous birthdays, as you were on your travels."

"An odd gadget certainly," Emily said, studying the instrument that Broderick placed so carefully upon the nearest table. She sniffed. "Is it quite useful then?"

"Excessively!" Broderick told her with a you-shouldn't-have glance in Rosemary's direction.

"What does it do?" Emily asked.

"It's rather like a magic tube, Gran," Rosemary explained. "It allows one to see into other worlds." Emily, her eyebrows raised, turned to Broderick for confirmation.

"Er . . . yes . . . it does do that," he replied hesitantly, as though uncertain of whether or not he agreed fully with Rosemary's word choice. "Actually, it enables the human eye to see the dimension of tiny wonders that surrounds us."

Observing Emily's confusion, he offered to set up the microscope and give a demonstration. His excitement was so contagious that Emily expressed a willingness to see for herself the wonders that would soon unfold before her very eyes. With a touching eagerness to share his scholastic enthusiasms, Broderick immediately proceeded to assemble the microscope with Gordon's able assistance.

"Far more complex than the old Van Leeuwenhoek model that I have in my study," Gordon noted aloud, to no one in particular. "Where'd you come by it?"

"I had Shumway look into having one made to order by a spectacles maker in London." Rosemary was clearly delighted by Broderick's apparent pleasure. "I understand that they are all the crack with the scholarly set, and I wanted Rick to have one of his own."

Broderick turned then to Rosemary, who was hovering attentively at his elbow, and took her two small white hands between his larger, brown ones. "Rosie, I can't thank you enough," he said softly. "It's too generous by half."

"Enough chattering!" Emily commanded, completely unaware of the gratified yet coy smile Rosemary had bestowed upon her childhood friend. "Let's have that demonstration you promised." Had she not been so impatient, Emily would have seen the satisfied gleam in her granddaughter's eyes and would have realized that Rosemary had, in no small way, successfully launched her scheme.

For the next hour, the party passed the time agreeably peering into the lens at various items, which Broderick carefully placed upon small plates of glass: A drop of wine, a thread of wool, and later, when tea had been served, sugar crystals. Mr. Loren even took a few scrapings from his strong, white teeth and allowed Mrs. Addison and Rosemary to examine the scrapings through the amazing instrument.

"What are those wriggling things?" Emily asked, peering into the lens. She stepped aside to allow her granddaughter to view them as well.

"Anton Van Leeuwenhoek called them 'little beasties,' " Broderick told her with a boyish grin. "We know them as *bacteria.*"

Without further encouragement, the young scholar launched into such a lively lecture upon the subject that Rosemary, seeing a side of her longtime friend that she had not been aware of, thought what a wonderful professor he would make. They all enjoyed an animated discussion of science and its benefits for mankind, until Emily, noting the time, called for her carriage.

"Rosemary is supposed to be on a repairing lease," she said lightly. "Her mother would not approve of such late hours. All this excitement quite defeats the purpose of our journey."

"Don't try to gammon me, Emily Addison!" Gordon warned her with a conspiratorial wink. "The gel is obviously in the bloom of good health. And so are you, if I may be so bold to mention it!"

"Looks can be quite deceiving," Emily said crushingly, as she followed her host to the door, and allowed him to assist her with her shawl. A slight flush of color in her cheeks, however, testified to her pleasure at the compliment.

Rosemary took advantage of this exchange of pleasantries to pull the unsuspecting Broderick aside in the hall. "Ricky, I must see you tomorrow on a matter of *great importance*," she confided in hushed tones. "Will you go riding with me in the morning?"

"If you wish it," Broderick agreed cordially. "These are yours, I believe," and he handed her two white gloves that she had unknowingly abandoned in the drawing room.

"You won't forget? Tomorrow morning," she reminded him in low but urgent tones. If she couldn't rely on Rick, who could she rely on? He'd been like a brother to her over the years—getting her out of childish scrapes and sneaking confections to her when she was being punished with a bread and water diet. Rosemary was counting on his assistance now more desperately than ever before.

Frowning slightly, Broderick simply nodded as Uncle Gordon took Rosemary's hand and assisted her into the carriage. Sinking back upon the cushions, Rosemary gave a ragged sigh of relief. She conjured the image of Lord Beverley's handsome face and sighed again. There had been a small army of heiresses and determined mothers over the years who'd tried to snare the dashing earl and failed. Rosemary was determined to succeed. It would be a feather in her cap, certainly, and she would be the envy of all the females in London. As Lady Beverley she would enjoy a life of adventure and privilege. Her plan was now in motion, and with Broderick's cooperation, she would soon become the blushing bride of the handsome and elusive Thomas Alden, Lord Beverley!

Chapter Three

The next morning, Broderick, dressed in buckskin breeches and glossy riding boots, sat down to a hearty breakfast, although afterwards, he could not have told anyone what he had tasted. He was so perplexed by Rosemary's sense of urgency in wishing to speak with him that he had not slept very well during the night. His stern face, void of the boyish charm that it had manifested last evening, provoked Mr. Gordon Stanley-Hodge to anger.

"Damn me if I understand your milk-toast generation!" the old gentleman declared heatedly as he attacked a rasher of bacon. "Puddingheads, every one of you! Why, in my day, when a gentleman planned to go riding with a beautiful gel, he didn't come down to breakfast looking as though he suffered with a liver complaint!"

Glaring at his protege, he stabbed the air with his fork. "Rosemary Addison is the prettiest female I've clapped eyes on in an age. If you had any sense at all, you young jackanapes, you'd ask the gel to marry you!"

Broderick looked up from his plate with an expression of complete abstraction. "I beg your pardon," he replied vaguely. "I was not attending."

Gordon snorted contemptuously. "I said that if you had one ounce of common sense in that muttonhead of yours, you would make Rosemary an offer!"

Broderick's eyes widened with panic. "An offer?" he choked. "Of marriage?"

"Of course marriage, you numbskull!" The elderly man slammed his fist upon the table. "You think I'd let you offer the girl a *carte blanche*?" The wealthy eccentric narrowed his grey eyes. "What's the matter with you, Broderick? Rosie is a ravishing beauty, and as rich as Croesus. As her husband, you would never find it necessary to exercise stringent economies. You could travel, buy dozens of microscopes, build half a dozen greenhouses, if you'd a mind to."

Daunted by the idea of marriage to Rosemary Addison, or to any other female for that matter, Broderick nearly dropped his fork. "I'm sure Rosemary would *scarcely* consider an offer from me," he said in a tight voice, his gaze fastened to the smeared surface of his plate.

"And why not? You're as well born as she is. And you've known one another since you were children. You get on well together, and I'm sure Rosebud has formed no lasting attachments in London—as yet. So, I repeat, why not?" the old man barked.

Broderick winced. "I'm sure it would be in Miss Addison's best interests to make a . . . a more advantageous connection."

"Bah! Rosie doesn't give a fig about connections!" Gordon said warmly. "The two of you would suit admirably, I'm certain of it."

Pausing abruptly, he regarded his protege with a considering glance. "Unless, of course, *your* affections are engaged elsewhere."

"No, they are not," Broderick responded, flushing. *And well you know it*, he wanted to shout, but his courteous manner prevented him from doing so.

Broderick had never really had an inclination to pursue women, and when he'd finally become aware of their singular charms, he found he had no time and certainly very little money for amorous pursuits. On the whole, he found females a crushing bore—always interested in their coiffures and fancy furbelows and never matters of consequence. As he had no fortune—only the modest annuity that Mr. Stanley-Hodge had purchased for him—and as his habits were considered eccentric and he considered his countenance ordinary, Broderick believed himself to be no matrimonial prize.

He would concede, however, that Rosemary Addison was the most personable female of his meager acquaintance. She was as lively as she was lovely—and had always been a good friend and a sympathetic listener, even when he chose to bore her with his scholastic interests. Broderick could not deny that he enjoyed her company, appreciated her wit, and was now—unexpectedly—awed by her beauty. But to make her an offer was absolutely out of the question!

Disturbing thoughts such as these plagued Broderick as he rode over to Oakley Manor and presented himself obligingly, although reluctantly, upon the doorstep. Rosemary, breathtaking in a bottle-green riding habit and a fetching little hat of the same color, greeted him with warm enthusiasm. The two enjoyed a long, brisk ride together through the countryside, as they had done many times before over the years. The meadow grass was sweet, the breeze was playful and Rosemary, with a contented sigh, remarked how much more enjoyable it was to ride in the country than in the confines of Hyde Park.

Later, they dismounted beside a small stream bordered by wild, purple iris and yellow buttercups. Broderick, both wishing for and dreading Rosemary's confidences, tied the horses to a small tree and walked beside the young heiress in silence.

"Ricky, I need your help," she said at last, turning pleading eyes upon his impassive face.

"I'm at your service," he replied chivalrously, if not eagerly. "What kind of scrape do you find yourself in now?"

"Oh, it's nothing of that sort. I . . . I want us to become

engaged—just temporarily—and then I'll cry off," Rosemary added hastily as she perceived the shock Broderick had sustained by her unexpected announcement. "It would only be a temporary arrangement," she assured him," and I wouldn't ask you to . . . to endure it if it wasn't *absolutely necessary.*"

"Good God!" Broderick declared in tones of extreme abhorrence. "Where have your wits gone a'begging, Rosie?"

Ignoring this unflattering exclamation, Rosemary gripped Broderick's coat sleeve. "Rick, don't be so stuffy! I'm desperate! It wouldn't be a *real* engagement. We need only keep up the pretense until Lord Beverley asks me to marry him."

"What? What kind of man would offer marriage to an *engaged* female? Sounds like a slow top to me . . . or worse!"

"He's not either! He's simply proud, that's all. I *know* he has every intention of marrying me, just as *I* have every intention of marrying *him.* But he needs to be taught a lesson," she added, a spot of color burning on each cheek. "He has humiliated me, and I want to teach him a lesson."

Rosemary then proceeded to tell the horrified Broderick her plan to bring the elusive earl to heel. And then, because Broderick was her oldest and dearest friend, she confided to him everything—the embarrassing conversation she had overheard in the garden, her mother's intention to see Rosemary wed before her bridal trip to India, and, finally, her outrageous plan to capture Lord Beverley's affectionate proposal of marriage.

"It won't fudge, Rosie. For one thing, no one would believe that a nonpareil like you would marry a . . . a rustic like me. Your clever earl will know it's all a hum. Why not coax one of your lovelorn London swells into participating in this cockeyed scheme of yours?" He strode fiercely along the path that followed the stream. Rosemary had to take several hurried, skipping steps in order to keep up with him.

"Anyone else would hold me to the engagement, that's why! I've been courted and odiously flattered by every fortune hunter in London."

Her blue eyes glittered dangerously with unshed tears. The thought of Thomas Alden's lack of amorous cooperation both hurt and angered her. He spent a great deal of time with her and was a generous suitor—all within the bounds of decorum. She'd expected him to propose marriage a year ago. So had her mother. Why had he not? Rosemary stopped skipping then and stood very still on the bank of the stream. She blinked back the tears that threatened to spill down her cheeks. Broderick, observing that he had left his beautiful but raving companion behind, stopped abruptly and turned back. His eyes, following her tearful gaze, briefly watched the water glistening in the sunshine.

"My fortune has become a great mortification to me," Rosemary said quietly.

"Whatever do you mean?" Broderick asked impatiently. Rosie wasn't making much sense. One minute she was proposing a mad scheme that could only land her in hot water and the next minute she was bemoaning her fortune! A great mortification indeed! Broderick wished he could be only half as mortified as Rosemary!

"Don't you see, Ricky?" the reluctant heiress said, turning to him with an anguished face that dissolved his anger and immediately made him feel all knotted up inside. "I will never really know *true love*. I'm pursued for my fortune and, to some extent, for my face, but not for myself. Even Beverley"—she looked down in embarrassment at the toes of her boots—"needs to marry for money. His pockets are let. He *must* marry an heiress. Fortunately, he's fixed his attention upon me."

"But do you love him, Rosie?" Broderick asked softly. He watched his young friend's face turn a becoming shade of pink.

"What a shocking romantic you are, Ricky!" she declared, glancing down at her hands. "Of course I love him!" Rosemary remembered the way her heart hammered against her ribs whenever Thomas was near her, whenever he led her to the dance floor or regarded her with those piercing blue eyes that seemed to penetrate the very fabric of her gown, in a most disconcerting but delicious manner. She sighed most audibly.

"Yes, I love him," she repeated. Glancing up again, Rosemary noted the unexpectedly tender expression on

Broderick's face. She pressed her advantage. "Please, Ricky, please say you'll do it! I'll do anything you like in return. I'll transfer funds from my account into yours," she began, "or finance your return expedition to America or buy you another microscope—anything!"

"Gads, Rosie! You needn't bribe me!" Broderick said, wincing. "If I help you with this ramshackle scheme of yours—and I said *if*—I'd do it because we're friends, because—"

"Oh, Rick! You're so gallant!" Rosemary flung her arms around the unsuspecting gentleman's neck and planted an enthusiastic kiss upon his left cheek.

Broderick recoiled from the sudden impact and the unexpected, though not unpleasant, shock. But Rosemary lost her balance, falling heavily against him and Broderick was forced to throw his arms around her in an effort to maintain his own. The surprising softness of her supple curves pressed against his own lithe, well-muscled form was rather staggering. Broderick realized, for the first time, that Rosemary Addison was no longer a child. He found himself silently cursing that laggard, Lord Beverley.

"Oh, Ricky, you will do it for me, won't you?" Rosemary pleaded, clinging to the lapels of his coat.

Broderick looked down into the young heiress' eyes that sparkled with hope. Tearing his eyes from the beguiling beauty mark upon her cheek, he groaned and reluctantly agreed to participate in Rosemary's scatter-brained scheme.

"I'll do it, Rosemary, but we've got to work out the details carefully." He pushed her away from him gently, but firmly. "We must—"

"Oh, I have already taken care of all the *tiniest* details," Rosemary told him happily. "You and I will enjoy one another's company constantly for the next few days, during which time, we will discover that we have a considerable *tendre* for one another. We will become engaged. I will tell my grandmother and we shall return to London to break the news to my mother."

"No doubt your mother will be quite taken aback by this," Broderick told her with a humorless smile.

"Oh, Mama will be *somewhat* surprised, but she won't protest. She's too eager to marry her dear Mr. Nevin. Besides, she likes you, Rick. She thinks you're quiet and unassuming."

Broderick tried not to clench his teeth. Quiet and unassuming, indeed! The perfect deportment for a young gentleman left in indigent circumstances by an improvident parent!

"She will give her approval," Rosemary continued, unaware of Broderick's smoldering resentment. "And the usual announcement will appear in *The Gazette*. Then you can join us in London for—"

"London!" her reluctant fiancé declared. "I can't go to London now! I have specimens to catalogue, cuttings to transplant. I—"

"It will only be for a few weeks. Everyone will want to meet you, of course. We will convince them that you and I have been childhood sweethearts, that I have declined all offers of marriage in hopes that *you* would ask for my hand upon your return from America."

"And then?" Broderick asked glumly. He was already resenting his chivalrous acceptance of Rosemary's harebrained plan. The thought of going to Almack's and the endless round of crushes and squeezes he would be forced to endure soured his good intentions. "What then?"

"Then the tardy Lord Beverley, realizing how much he loves me and desires me to be his wife, will succeed in convincing me of it!" Rosemary told him happily. "Realizing then that I truly love *him* and nurture only the deepest friendship for *you*, I will cry off and marry Thomas. You will retire to the country to lick your wounds and then quietly book passage to Botany Bay to immerse yourself in your studies."

A slow, appreciative grin transformed Broderick's gloomy visage. "Botany Bay! *That* sounds like the best part of the entire scheme. I've always wanted to go to Australia."

"And so you shall! At *my* expense. It's the *least* I can do after putting you to so much trouble." Rosemary slipped one of her small, expensively gloved hands into Broderick's larger ones. She gave it a squeeze and smiled up at him gratefully.

He shook his dark head and smiled at her dubiously. As he turned back toward the horses, Rosemary fell into step beside him. "But what if your elusive earl doesn't play the role of jealous lover?" he asked her, a slight frown furrowing his brow.

"Oh, he *will*," Rosemary said with more confidence than she actually felt. "I expect him to propose an elopement to the border almost immediately." She giggled then, enjoying the image of his lordship's aristocratic nose out of joint when Rosemary's engagement was announced, his subsequent wrath, and the passionate entreaties that would follow. "Of course, you must promise not to confide in Uncle Gordon," Rosemary told Broderick then, as an afterthought. "He's not a stickler but I believe he would consider my plan . . . not quite the thing."

"You're right there!" Broderick declared emphatically, recalling the critical peal Gordon had rung over his head at breakfast. If the eccentric old gentleman considered his protegee a numbskull for not proposing marriage to Miss Addison, what would he say should he learn of Broderick's compliance with her scheme to ensnare the Earl of Beverley into matrimony?

"Yes, I'm afraid that he'll just have to be taken in like everyone else!" Rosemary insisted. "It's much . . . much safer that way."

Safe? thought Broderick with considerable misgivings. He couldn't see that there was anything safe—or sane—about Rosemary's scheme. A hostile, jealous peer, the possibility of a duel, pistols at dawn! No, thought Broderick grimly, the plan was not safe at all!

Chapter Four

Broderick politely declined Mrs. Emily Addison's invitation to stay for luncheon, insisting that Tupp needed his assistance in the greenhouse. But Broderick did promise to return later that afternoon.

"Bring Gordon with you," Emily commanded. "I want to hear more of your voyage to America. Perhaps your experiences would be of some benefit to me in my writing," she added, too engrossed in other matters to note Broderick's uplifted eyebrow and the amused glance he cast in Rosemary's direction.

After Broderick returned to the Hall, Rosemary went upstairs to change into an afternoon dress of apple-green muslin then joined her grandmother at the dining table where, over a light repast of cold meats, fresh fruits and an assortment of cheeses, the budding novelist entertained her granddaughter with various trials and triumphs of her morning's composition.

"I trust you can entertain yourself, dear, for I simply must return to my desk—the muse is most insistent!" Emily said with a dutiful sigh.

Rosemary assured her grandmother that she was quite capable of looking after her own amusement, and retired happily to a comfortable seat in the shady corner of the garden. There she eagerly continued her reading of *Camilla,* another delightful novel by the admirable Mrs. Burney.

She was mildly astonished to realize that she actually *enjoyed* reading. Of course, she seldom found time to do so during the hectic London season, but was quite content now to be alone with a good book. After many weeks with a frantic social schedule, it was simply delicious to sit still, absorbing the warmth of the afternoon sun pouring through the window. Rosemary appreciated her state of comfortable solitude. And she was confident now that, with Broderick's assistance, her plan to bring Lord Beverley to her upon his knees would surely succeed.

Later over tea, Fanny Burney and Ann Radcliffe were the topic of conversation—a topic introduced by Emily herself, who mentioned proudly that she, like these creative women, was writing a novel.

"I never even heard of 'em!" Gordon replied with gruff disapproval. "And I never read such dribble. Lud!

If I ever get through the piles of scholarly tomes I intend to read before I turn up my toes, I'll consider myself fortunate indeed."

"Uncle Gordon, don't tell me you've not even read Sir Walter Scott's *Waverley* or Mrs. Radcliffe's *Mysteries of Udolfo*?" Rosemary declared, incredulously. "Why, they are all the rage."

"Bah!" the elderly man barked. "Fairy tales for grownups, that's what they are! No meat, no substance!"

"Fairy tales?" said his hostess, taking considerable umbrage. "Novels are more than that, I'll have you know. They are, in point of fact, reflections of life—verbal portraits captured carefully with words rather than brushstrokes."

Emily then launched into a heated defense of the art form, while Rosemary glanced quickly over the tea tray, her blue eyes reflecting the amusement evident in Broderick's good-natured gaze. The smile that had been tugging at the corners of her lips emerged fully, and Broderick grinned back at her. His dark face was irresistibly attractive when illuminated by a boyish smile, Rosemary thought then. Reflecting briefly upon the disappointment the vicar's daughter would surely experience when she learned of Broderick Loren's engagement, Rosemary felt a twinge of guilt.

When Gordon and Emily paused in their lively debate of the novel's virtues, Rosemary quickly intervened by offering to refill their cups and by expressing her willingness to loan her volume of *Waverley* to her eccentric neighbor. He received Rosemary's gracious offer with an unappreciative snort.

"I'll wait for your grandmother's book to be published," he said in a tone that clearly indicated his disbelief that any such incident would occur.

Then noting the stiffening of Emily's already rigid spine and the slight flare of her delicate nostrils, Gordon added quickly, "I'm sure that whatever Emily has to say will be ever so much more to the point, although *why* you want to spend your time writing a novel is beyond my understanding."

"And why not?" Emily asked, helping herself to another lemon biscuit. "And besides," she added more thoughtfully, "I have nothing better to do—other than seeing that Rosemary is comfortably settled in a suitable matrimonial arrangement, and even that, strictly speaking, is my daughter-in-law's responsibility."

If Emily noted the heightened color of Rosemary's cheeks at that moment or the slow flush that tinged Broderick's tanned countenance, she did not comment upon either.

"Broderick, *you* would care to borrow *Waverley,* would you not?" she asked. "Or perhaps one of Mrs. Burney's novels? I think you will not find them dull, even though you have chosen to remain rather aloof from society at large."

"Of course he would enjoy it!" Rosemary answered for him. "Rick is a true scholar"—and here she threw

Gordon a challenging glare—"and *he* must surely feel the need to expose himself to new and various ideas."

"Er . . . yes," Broderick replied uncertainly. "This is a particularly hectic time for me, however, having just returned from our long journey. There are specimens to be transplanted and cataloged and—"

He stopped abruptly, observing the disappointment on Rosemary's lovely face and then took note of Mrs. Addison's disapproving glare. "But . . . er . . . perhaps I could read a chapter each evening before retiring," he hastened.

"My field journal would be more interesting than some tittle-tattle written by a gentlewoman!" Gordon declared impatiently.

Before Broderick or Rosemary could intervene, Emily stepped up to the challenge. Yet another heated debate ensued. When verbally exhausted, the two adversaries ceased their argument. Broderick quickly took advantage of the lull to suggest that he and Gordon take their leave, allowing Mrs. Addison to return to her writing. Rosemary quietly slipped away to retrieve the promised book for her friend and handed it to him as he was preparing to depart. The heiress noted, with carefully concealed amusement, that Broderick accepted the volume manfully.

"Don't you read anything other than the scientific?" she asked him, tilting her honey-gold head to one side invitingly.

"Of course I do! I frequently read philosophy, the

classics, and even Shakespeare. And if you must know, I enjoy a comic streak as well and am rather fond of Ovid's *Metamorphoses*."

"Tell me about it," she said encouragingly.

"Ovid? He relates the escapades—amorous and otherwise—of the gods and particular mortals."

"Oh, the ancients!" Rosemary said knowingly. "Should I like it, do you think?"

Broderick grinned down at her briefly. Then, as he recalled some of the more titillating tales, he managed to frown. "No doubt you *would*—although you *shouldn't*!" he said severely, as though finding fault with her character. "I daresay neither your mother or your grandmother would approve of the subject matter. Besides, it's in Latin."

"Why, Rick, you could read them to me!" Rosemary suggested, wanting very much to hear any tales that her mother would disapprove of. The girl then gurgled with pleasure as she observed Broderick's shocked expression.

"I think not!" he declared shortly.

"Then, as you do not care to read to me, shall we go riding again tomorrow morning?" She offered him her hand in farewell. It would not do to set Broderick's back up so that he felt himself obliged to renege on his agreement. Besides, it was necessary that she and Broderick spend as much time together as possible, so that the imminent engagement would be a believable one.

"Yes, I shall ride over for you in the morning."

But Rosemary could not help but notice the absence of enthusiasm in his voice. For a brief moment, she felt remorseful that she had embroiled her reclusive friend into such a deceptive plot. But when Rosemary considered her goal—to marry Lord Beverley, whom she adored with all her young heart—she ignored her qualms and decided that Broderick should be pleased to help her achieve so important an objective!

And so the following morning, and the morning after that, Broderick rode about the countryside, dutifully accompanying the lovely Miss Addison. Rosemary, determined to ensure that her reluctant friend should not regret his agreement to pose as her fiancé, was on her best behaviour—personable, lively, and attentive. She encouraged him to talk about his interests, and when he invited her to the Hall to view further articles of interest beneath the much-appreciated microscope, she accepted.

"I'd like to, above all things!" Rosemary declared, perjuring herself without hesitation. She had to please Broderick, to humor him. After all, it was the least she could do after coercing him into her deceptive scheme.

Willingly, she followed Broderick to his book-lined study and submitted herself to the viewing of a bee's stinger, a few grains of pollen from a lily and the scales of a butterfly's wing through the magnifying lenses of his new microscope. So interesting was Broderick's discourse that Rosemary again found herself wondering if her friend should seek a post at one of the universities. Once Uncle Gordon died, and his property passed on to his heir—a spineless nephew cursed with gout and a waspish wife—then Broderick would be forced to find a home elsewhere, as well as occupation. A university post would be most suitable.

"I believe you would enjoy making the acquaintance of Sir Halsey Paige," Rosemary murmured, her eye fixed thoughtfully upon the viewing lens. "It is my understanding that he is—"

"I know well who he is! But do *you* know the gentleman? Would it be possible for you to arrange an introduction?" Broderick's face was animated by eager anticipation.

Rosemary noted the excitement in his glowing brown eyes—eyes attractively fringed with long, thick lashes. She was touched by his enthusiasm.

"I've never met him myself," she confessed. The scholarly baronet was as eccentric as Uncle Gordon and nearly as reclusive. "But his granddaughter Clarissa is a particular friend of mine, so I'm sure that something could be arranged."

Broderick laughed delightedly. "That would be wonderful! It would make my part in your little charade completely worthwhile."

"What? You mean that merely meeting this gentleman—who's rumored to be *completely* off his head—would satisfy you?" Rosemary asked, a teasing glint in her eye. "I would not need to finance your voyage to Botany Bay?"

"Off his head? Is that the conclusion of your London

ton? Why, the man is a genius! A fearless pioneer in the field of botany!"

Before Rosemary could divert him with further playful banter, Broderick proceeded to relate one anecdote after another regarding the botanical triumphs of Sir Halsey. This animated discourse naturally led Broderick to escort Rosemary through his greenhouse—the pride and joy of his existence. Rosemary, eager to comply with his every whim, followed him dutifully. Broderick had made considerable improvements since her last visit years ago, and Rosemary was surprised.

"Why, Ricky! This is extraordinary!" She was amazed at the number of plant specimens, as well as the wide variety that had been collected and so attractively displayed.

He introduced Tupp, his greenhouse gardener—a thin, ginger-haired man.

"Pleased to meet you, miss," Tupp murmured self-consciously, his Adam's apple bobbing up and down his throat in a disconcerting manner.

Rosemary nodded politely and watched with interest as Tupp deftly plugged a small plant into a bed of dirt. Strolling down one small aisle after another, with Broderick following behind, the heiress was speechless with admiration. Rosemary also felt a flicker of pride.

"I am impressed, truly!" she told him. "I can well imagine the considerable effort and expense that have gone into this hobby of yours."

"It's not a hobby," Broderick contradicted, but not impolitely. "It is my life."

Watching the glow of his face, the gleam in his eyes, Rosemary suddenly understood what a sacrifice he would be making, on her behalf, when he left the country to pose as her betrothed in London. She felt another twinge of guilt. But before she could say anything to the point, Gordon, his white hair standing out around his head like a windblown halo, joined them in front of a display of giant ferns.

"Has our Mr. Buds been boring you to tears with his chatter of blossoms, Rosie?" the elderly man greeted her, taking possession of the small gloved hand that Rosemary held out to him.

"I am *not* bored," she assured him and was considerably astonished to realize that indeed she was not. "I am, however, overwhelmed. And you, Uncle Gordon, do not fool me one bit!" She pulled her hand from his affectionate grasp with a missish air. "I know you're as proud of Ricky's achievement as I am."

Gordon chuckled hoarsely. He would not admit that what Rosemary said was true. Having never married nor fathered a family of his own, Broderick Loren was like a son to him. And although loathe to admit it, Gordon was fonder of Broderick and prouder of his abilities than he ever thought he could be when the parentless child was thrust upon him as an unwelcome ward so many years ago.

The elderly scholar ambled over to a cluster of blooming orchids and glanced down at them appreciatively. "I suppose it *is* rather interesting," he said dryly, shrugging his shoulders.

"Not, of course, as interesting as beetles, but still— these do hold some fascination." He indicated the exotic blossoms with an impatient wave of his hand. "Has Broderick shown you these little gems? He brought them back from the islands."

Rosemary joined Gordon in admiration of the orchids. A small sigh of appreciation escaped her lips. "Lovely! And look! This one is the very color of my glove!" In saying so, Rosemary thrust forward one hand, encased in a pale lavender kid glove, so that the men might make the comparison for themselves.

"Indeed it is!" Gordon noted. "There you go, Broderick! That's the very name for this little beauty— Rosemary's Glove!"

Broderick grinned and nodded. Rosemary turned her wide-eyed gaze upon one gentleman and then the other. "Why, is that how one goes about naming a flower? Mercly by whim?" she asked, astonished.

"Not exactly," Broderick replied. "We use the method adopted by Carolus Linnaeus—the Swedish botanist."

He then explained this means of taxonomic classification in the simplest of terms, and showed the young heiress his catalogue of recorded specimens. "And so while an apple is called a *Pyrus malus*, a pear is a *Pyrus communicus*," he threw in, by way of example.

"What, then, is the Latin name for this particular orchid?" Rosemary asked.

Broderick glanced over her head at his grinning mentor and raised his dark brown eyebrows. "I am not certain. You see, it's my belief that this orchid has never before been catalogued or named. Gordon discovered it while we were tramping about on one of our collecting expeditions. If a similar specimen has never before been discovered, then I am the fortunate individual who is allowed the privilege of naming this one!"

"Oh, *do* name it Rosemary's Glove!" the excited heiress pleaded. "I should feel so honored if you'd do so!" She glanced lovingly down at the pale lavender bloom.

Gordon snorted. "What? A diamond of the first water like yourself—one who has no doubt received any number of love poems and other tributes tied up with gilded ribbon—and you desire to have a silly flower named after your glove?"

"It is as you say," Rosemary replied matter-of-factly and without conceit. "I have received ever so many tributes, as you call them. But to have an exotic flower named after my glove is a far superior triumph, I can assure you. So much more gratifying than the ordinary sort!"

It suddenly mattered . . . it mattered a great deal. Turning to Broderick, she fixed him with her sparkling blue gaze. "Do say you will name it after my glove, Ricky. *Do!*"

"We shall see," her friend replied indulgently. "This little beauty may already have a name. I may simply be unaware of it for the time being. It is my responsibility to be certain."

"Bah! Enough about blossoms!" Gordon declared. "Come look at my beetles, Rosebud. I've made a few impressive additions since last you visited us before we left."

The elderly gentleman offered Rosemary his arm and the young heiress accepted it with a warm smile and followed him out of the greenhouse and to his own scholarly sanctuary. The Beetle Room, as Rosemary had called it as a child, retained its familiar odors of musty books, beeswax and lemon oil. Both the aroma and the organized clutter brought back fond memories of rainy afternoons spent here in this very room. Glass cases containing an astonishing collection of beetles were the main focal point. In each case, beetles in various stages—eggs, grubs, pupas and adults—were interestingly displayed.

Rosemary, glancing now at Uncle Gordon's newest specimens and listening to him elucidate his favorite subject, could remember having felt a bit sorry for the poor dead creatures pinned so finally into their designated places upon the velvet inside the cases. She could also recall her wide-eyed astonishment when Uncle Gordon had told her approximately how many kinds of beetles God had placed upon the earth.

"Why, Rosebud, I daresay you could study a different

beetle each day for the next fifty years and you would still not have studied them all!" he had said proudly, as though personally responsible for this incredible circumstance.

"You've certainly increased your collection," Rosemary spoke up then, as Uncle Gordon paused for breath in the midst of his enthusiastic expounding.

"Yes, and let me show you this little gem," he said, grasping Rosemary by the elbow and leading her to the desk where a variety of specimens were pinned to stiff paper, waiting to be properly cataloged and displayed. "Ain't it a beauty!" the man declared admiringly, indicating a particularly deadly looking specimen.

"It's called a unicorn beetle—a gentleman in Nassau presented it to me when he learned of my predilection for such creatures. Do you see the horn there in the center of its head?"

Rosemary regarded the unicorn beetle with interest. Later, after having examined all of the latest additions, she graciously accepted Uncle Gordon's offer of a glass of sherry.

"Cook will be pleased," Broderick told her. "She heard that you were visiting this afternoon, and it's my understanding that she planned to make fig cakes just for you."

"How thoughtful!" Rosemary declared, touched by the woman's remembering her childhood passion for the pastries. "I only hope Gran isn't too worried about me."

"Bah!" Gordon said with a dismissing grunt. "Emily

will be so absorbed in her scribbling that she won't
have noticed the time. Novel writing, indeed! It's an odd
employment, I must say. Why she should occupy herself with it, I cannot understand."

Rosemary, a smile quivering upon her lips, looked up
to find Broderick's glinting brown eyes fixed upon her
with amusement. He had a delightful understanding of
the ridiculous, she realized, and wondered how he would
get on in London, where many of the fashionable amusements would afford considerable ridiculousness to appreciate. Rosemary realized, too, that she was actually
looking forward to sharing the adventure with him.

"Fiddlesticks!" she declared with a gurgle of laughter. "Writing a novel is not any more unusual than collecting beetles and rare blossoms. Far less so, I should
think," she added as a young footman came in carrying
the heavy tea tray.

Broderick, happily recalling Rosemary's promise to
arrange an introduction to Sir Halsey, was on the verge
of sharing this exciting bit of news with Gordon when
he suddenly realized that he could not do so without revealing Rosemary's scheme to ensnare the elusive Earl
of Beverley. He shut his mouth abruptly and thought
again of the idiocy of Rosemary's entire plan.

Later, as he rode with her back to Oakley Manor, his
grim expression must have reflected his thoughts. Rosemary, glancing at his somber expression, seemed able to
read his mind.

"I daresay you'll be wishing me at Jericho before

this is all over and done with," she said with a rueful smile, "but I *do* hope you are not considering backing out of our agreement."

"No, I wouldn't do that," Broderick said, slightly annoyed. He had, after all, given his word as a gentleman. "The sooner I get to London, the sooner I can return to Hodge Hall."

"And the sooner you will have the opportunity to meet your illustrious botanist," Rosemary reminded him temptingly.

"Yes, Sir Halsey Paige," Broderick replied absently. "Let's get on with it then, shall we? When will you tell your grandmother that we're engaged?"

"*I* shall not tell Gran—we shall tell her together, and soon. But if it is to be believable, we must spend considerable time in one another's pockets, you know. And you must be more like a lover in your attentions to me."

Rosemary noted the slow flush, which colored Broderick's tanned cheeks. Her lips twitched with amusement at his discomfort. "I promise you, it will not be so very unpleasant. I'm considered a desirable companion. I will not repulse you. Perhaps, at the first of next week, we shall be able to announce our intentions to my grandmother."

Rosemary smiled at her friend then—a dazzling smile that had been known to bring stronger men to their knees—literally. Even the most critical observer would have declared her a piece of perfection. The effect of this loveliness upon poor Broderick—unused as he was to such perfection—was devastating. He felt his pulse race and swallowed back a thick lump in his throat.

"You'll be well recompensed for your part in my little scheme," Rosemary said, leaning towards him in the saddle. Placing one of her gloved hands over his own, she added, "I promise, you'll not be sorry, Ricky." She released his hand then and kicked her mount forward, moving ahead of Broderick along the path.

Broderick found the intimate gesture to be almost physically painful. His breath came now in irregular spurts. He found himself thinking, once again, what a fool Lord Beverley was.

"Sorry?" he murmured thickly, watching Rosemary's retreating form. "I'm sorry already, and the charade has yet to begin!"

Chapter Five

"You must stop all this gadding about, my dear! You are on a repairing lease, or so we have told your mama. It will never do to return to London looking like a hag."

Emily Addison's cheery tone eliminated the sting from her scolding. Attractively attired in a morning gown of dove-grey silk and wearing a frilly cap set pertly upon her silver-white curls, the widow sat beside a sunny window at the simple pedestal table composing a new chapter for her novel.

Unmoved by her grandmother's rebuke, Rosemary smiled at her affectionately before turning her attention again to several letters which had arrived in the morning post. Not one of them was from Lord Beverley, she noted with dismay. In the past three weeks, she had received only one brief missive from that elusive peer, forwarded by her mother. Chagrined, Rosemary was more determined than ever to make Thomas Alden, the Earl of Beverley, regret his indifference.

"What news have you?" her grandmother asked, interrupting Rosemary's unchristian contemplations.

"According to Mama, the weather in town has been unseasonably warm. The cook succumbed to heat exhaustion and has been ordered to bed. Mama is quite distraught."

"So would I be if I had succumbed to the heat!" her grandmother declared with some feeling, looking up from her manuscript.

"No, Gran, *the cook* succumbed—Mama is merely distraught. My friend Clarissa writes that one of Sir John Knetley's handsome greys broke a leg and had to be put down. She adds that it is so hot that the ices from Gunther's melt into unsightly puddles before one can eat them. Clarissa misses me and wishes I would return to London as soon as possible. So, apparently, do all my beaus."

The heiress displayed several fervent appeals for her to make haste to return to London.

"How very thoughtless, to be sure!" Emily declared, her quill poised above her sheet of foolscap. "Everyone and everything in the city is melting, by all accounts. Why should we return when we are so very comfortable here at Oakley?"

"Indeed! I'm in no hurry to return to London! Why, I can't recall when I've so enjoyed a stay in the country!"

In truth, Rosemary was having a wonderful time. Broderick had proven to be an amiable companion, and she was enjoying their time together. She felt assured that her plan would go smoothly. The very thought of Lord Beverley's outrage caused her to shudder with delicious anticipation. However, for her grandmother's benefit, Rosemary tried to look bashful and even a little flustered.

Mrs. Addison, noting this missish demonstration, regarded her granddaughter suspiciously.

"Hmmm. I suppose you *are* enjoying yourself immensely. After all, young Broderick has been very attentive. He has quite monopolized your time," she noted dryly. "You *should* be resting and recuperating your strength."

"But I feel fine . . . now!" Rosemary protested meekly.

"I see that you do. But your distraught mama would not approve of your jaunting all over the countryside. Nor would she approve of your picking strawberries like some kitchen wench! I don't know what Broderick could have been thinking of to suggest such a thing!"

"It wasn't Ricky's idea! I insisted that he pull the curricle over so that I could watch the workers at their task. The berries looked so tempting, and the chore so quaint. I quite convinced him to allow me to try my hand at it."

"And Broderick complied." The twinkle in Emily's eye contradicted the sternness in her tone.

"Naturally." Rosemary smiled and dimpled prettily.

"The farmer who owned the field could not have been kinder. He even gave us a good rate on the baskets of berries we bought."

Mrs. Addison snorted. "But your gloves! Stained beyond repair!"

"No matter," Rosemary declared with a shrug. "I *quite* enjoyed myself!"

She was surprised to realize, in all sincerity, that she *had* found the outing a delightful one. Broderick had been good-natured about the whole incident. And Rosemary was convinced that the strawberry flummery served at dinner that evening tasted particularly delicious, since she had picked the berries herself.

"Gordon is equally to blame!" Emily went on crisply. "Careening all over the countryside in pursuit of a balloon, with you and Broderick urging him on."

"But, Gran! It was one of those *immense* balloons that is operated with hot air," Rosemary reminded her, as though this would alleviate her grandparent's disapproval. "The two gentlemen appreciated Uncle Gordon's assistance at their descent in Squire Feddleman's field. Ricky took the time to explain the valves and other gadgets to me and it was really quite fascinating!"

"Fascinating, indeed!" Unconvinced, Emily returned to her manuscript.

The next morning, as they enjoyed their daily ride together, Rosemary told Broderick: "Gran does not approve of all my gadding about."

"I know of something else she won't approve of either. I hope his lordship will eventually appreciate your efforts to save his pride," Broderick added, his tone waspish.

Rosemary remained silent. Lord Beverley would *not* appreciate her efforts in the least, she knew. She had already resolved that the proud but impoverished earl would never know to what lengths his bride had gone to ensure her happiness and his financial security.

"What's he like—Beverley, I mean?"

"Simply the most handsome and romantic man I know!" Rosemary declared with a happy glow. "Some have even compared him to the sort of wicked earls that are always main characters in the circulating library romances!"

When this description failed to impress her scholarly companion, Rosemary tried a different approach. "He's tall, attractive, witty and charming. He excels at all fashionable amusements and cuts a dashing figure in the ballroom. What more can I say? He's *man perfected*!"

"And a peer of the realm," Broderick threw in.

"Yes, that too," Rosemary said with a defensive jut of her small chin. "But he cannot be held responsible for his being born to a title, any more than my father could have been held accountable for being born without one!"

"I wasn't casting blame upon the man for his possession of a title. Does your mother favor the earl's suit?"

"Certainly. Mama has been hoping for some time that

his lordship would declare his intentions. She has set her heart on having a countess for a daughter."

"You, of course, care nothing for this privilege."

"Not a fig!" Rosemary affirmed proudly. "I love Thomas! I'd marry him if he were nothing more than a penniless curate!" After a moment's pause, she laughed. "Well, perhaps not. I do wonder sometimes about the dull life I shall lead as a married woman."

Broderick's light brown eyes began to twinkle. His lips quivered slightly. "What makes you assume that your life as Lady Beverley will be so dull?"

"Upon reflection, it must prove to be so," Rosemary answered vaguely. "From the moment my childish fingers were capable of holding a needle, I was taught the fine art of fancy work. And then came dancing lessons and deportment and music and art lessons."

"Worthy pursuits, all," Broderick declared with wry amusement.

"Worthy, certainly. But for what purpose? That of securing a husband. Once the nuptials have taken place, what is there for me to do?" She turned her doubtful gaze upon him. "Only more of the same, and this time, without the motivation. For I shall have secured my husband."

"If marriage is so depressing a state, then why do you wish to wed your wicked earl?"

"A girl *must* marry," Rosemary pointed out matter-of-factly. "And besides," she added, taking umbrage at Broderick's mocking glance, "I have feelings for Lord

Beverley, more so than for any other man I've ever met, so I might as well live a boring life with him as another."

"It needn't be boring," Broderick said in a more serious tone. "Two people who truly love each other—who are agreeably compatible—need never be bored in one another's company. With a sense of adventure, a man and wife can enjoy their life together."

Noting Rosemary's appraising expression, Broderick continued. "There are books to read and discuss, exotic countries to explore, interesting people to meet, and new friendships and studies to cultivate."

Rosemary chuckled. "I don't imagine that Lord Beverley will forsake his London cronies to explore foreign parts with me. And I cannot imagine him sitting in a library reading a book of any sort."

Reaching over for one of Broderick's hands, Rosemary clutched it tightly. "But I *shall* make him happy. I shall! Why, the needlework upon his slippers will be so exquisite that Thomas will be tempted to wear them in public so he may boast of my skill!" Rosemary declared laughingly. "And I'll fill the house with my gayest watercolors and practice Haydn and Giordani on my pianoforte every evening!"

"He'll find you quite accomplished, I'm sure," Broderick said quietly.

"And devoted," Rosemary added in a more frivolous tone. "For why else should I pursue such occupations, except to please *him*?"

When Broderick didn't respond, Rosemary led the

conversation down another path. "I think we should announce our betrothal to my grandmother upon our return."

"Today?" Broderick croaked. His hands tightened on the reins and his chestnut mare pranced nervously, sensitive to the change in its master's conduct.

"Yes, today," Rosemary said calmly. "You had not planned to keep me in the saddle until tomorrow, surely?" Her blue eyes glinted merrily as she noted her companion's sudden discomfort.

"Let's be quick about it then, before I lose what little courage I possess." Broderick hardened his features with grim determination.

"Ricky, you're roasting me!" Rosemary said gaily. "You're very courageous and clever. I've no doubt that we'll both pull off this charade with great aplomb."

Later, having returned to Oakley Manor to confront the elder Mrs. Addison, Rosemary wasn't so sure. She was nervous, and Broderick did not seem as composed as she'd hoped he would be. He appeared flushed and was slightly breathless when he addressed Rosemary's grandmother in the drawing room.

"I realize that this must come as a surprise to you, ma'am," he hastened to add after Rosemary revealed the startling news. "But as Rosie and I have been friends for so long, we did not feel the need to stand upon ceremony."

"I *am* rather surprised," Emily admitted, regarding a blushing Rosemary first and then Broderick.

"But not disapproving, I hope," he went on, playing his part admirably.

"*Please* give us your blessing, Gran," Rosemary pleaded, slipping an arm around her grandmother's waist.

"Gladys must be consulted, of course."

"Certainly. We shall return to London with all haste so that Broderick may place his suit before her. Only, I do hope you will encourage Mama to look upon the match favorably."

"I realize that I have no fortune, no title and no expectations," Broderick threw in. "But my affection for Rosie is sincere and has been of long duration. I did not hope that she would feel the same for me." He glanced sidelong at Rosemary, and his face turned slightly crimson beneath his tan. They had rehearsed this speech but still, he felt like a fool.

On cue, Rosemary slipped one of her small hands into Broderick's larger one, while caressing his coat sleeve with the other. "Ours is a love match, Gran. My fortune will more than make up for what Ricky does not possess, don't you agree?"

Emily returned her granddaughter's frank gaze with a skeptical one. "Your fortune is considerable, Rosemary, and you are certainly in a position to marry whom you want. I shall write to your mother immediately and demand that she come down to Oakley at once."

"There's no need. You and I shall return to London

and take Broderick with us. I want everyone to know of my complete happiness as soon as possible."

With those gushing words, the heiress turned a soulful gaze upon her betrothed and blushed prettily. She was confident that she appeared quite convincing. She hoped poor Broderick's obvious discomfort would be mistaken for shyness.

"No, I think your mother should come to Oakley," her grandmother contradicted. "Does Gordon know about this turn of events?" She turned shrewd eyes upon Broderick's flushed face.

"No, ma'am. Rosemary wanted you to be the first to know," he answered stiffly.

"You will wish us happy, won't you, Gran?" Rosemary asked, while mauling Broderick's sleeve in a fit of emotional agitation.

"Yes, my dear," her grandmother replied with the barest hint of a smile. Looking from one young person to the other, she said sincerely, "I wish you both very happy indeed."

Chapter Six

Whatever misgivings Emily Addison may have had concerning her granddaughter's unexpected engagement, she kept them to herself. A letter was promptly posted to Rosemary's unsuspecting mother in London, revealing the astonishing news and urging Gladys to hasten to Oakley at the earliest possible moment. If the elder Mrs. Addison had received the news of Rosemary's engagement somewhat skeptically, Gordon Stanley-Hodge was simply delighted. "Come here and give me a kiss, you little minx!" he demanded when she and Broderick broke the news to him. He planted a warm, affectionate kiss upon the heiress' blushing cheek and then extended his hand to his former ward.

"Damn me if I don't do something handsome for you both!" Gordon declared. He glowed with pleasure as he wrung Broderick's hand with undisguised enthusiasm. "When will you be leaving for London to seek Mrs. Addison's approval?"

"Actually, Mrs. Addison has written to Rosemary's mother requesting her presence at Oakley immediately," Broderick informed him with an embarrassed cough.

"When Mama arrives, we shall iron out all the details then," Rosemary quickly put in. She didn't relish the idea of trying to answer Gordon's questions about the wedding plans. "I'm quite sure Mama will have no objection. She'll be relieved to have me off her hands so she can marry her dear Mr. Nevin and journey with him to India this autumn."

Gordon chuckled at Rosemary's flippancy. He beamed upon the young couple with apparent pleasure. "Rosebud, you couldn't have made me happier! Why, I've more affection for you than any of my own relatives, and Broderick, you've been like a son to me."

In his delight, the old gentleman did not notice the heightened flush in Rosemary's cheeks or the guilty glint in Broderick's eyes. "This calls for a celebration, indeed it does!" and he ordered his butler to bring up a bottle of the best champagne.

When Gladys Addison arrived at Oakley Manor at the week's end, accompanied by the ever-attentive Mr. Edgar Nevin, she was too astonished by the news to register any emotion but that of complete surprise.

"Rosemary, dear, are you *certain* it is Broderick Loren you wish to marry?" she asked in a slightly puzzled tone.

Determined to play her part perfectly, and annoyed that her mother had not seen fit to hold this particular conversation with her in private, Rosemary cast a heated glare in Mr. Nevin's direction before answering firmly. "Indeed, I very much wish to marry Broderick. If I cannot marry Broderick Loren, I shall not marry at all!"

Rosemary observed Mr. Nevin's startled reaction to this declaration with a flush of satisfaction. Her mother blinked her eyes and wrung her hands. "I had no idea . . . I had not realized . . . that you and young Mr. Loren had any affection for one another."

"Indeed, we do." Rosemary thought her grandmother made an unladylike snort at that confession. But when she glanced in Emily's direction, Rosemary observed that lady studiously bent over her ever-lengthening manuscript and decided she must have imagined it.

"Broderick and I have been fond of one another for years and years, ever since we were children. It's only natural that our relationship should blossom into something more, er, something *more*."

"But I believed, I had hoped—" her nervous parent began before being rudely interrupted by a glowering Mr. Nevin.

"What difference does it make whom the girl marries?" he bellowed, causing Emily Addison to look up from her manuscript. "She need not marry a fortune— she has one of her own! And this Mr. Loren is, though impoverished, perfectly respectable, I believe."

"Perfectly," Rosemary answered coolly. She regarded

the man's thick, unhandsome features with raised eyebrows and a disapproving pucker of her lips. Her eyes
took on a dangerously smoky hue. She found herself
making unfavorable comparisons of his solid, portly
frame to Broderick's tall, lithe one.

"This is all so sudden, my dear," Gladys protested
weakly. "I wish you to marry whom you will, but I do not
wish you to form a misalliance."

"Rosie is a sensible girl," Emily threw in.

Pleased by her grandmother's support, Rosemary
flashed her a grateful smile and said, "Rick and I have
known each other for quite some time. We suit admirably."

"There now, Gladys! They suit admirably!" Mr. Nevin
echoed. "Put your mind at rest, and give the girl your
blessing." Turning to Rosemary, he said brusquely, "I
daresay this Loren fellow is about somewhere, ready to
address your mother formally upon the matter?"

Rosemary nodded stiffly. "He and Mr. Gordon
Stanley-Hodge will be joining us for dinner this evening, at which time Broderick will wish to speak with
you, Mama, privately—alone." She emphasized 'privately' and 'alone,' while wondering how the intrusive
Mr. Nevin had maintained his position with the diplo-
matic corps through the years.

Gordon wondered the same when he and Broderick
were introduced to the gentleman upon their arrival at
Oakley that evening.

"Don't see why we must keep up any pretense of for-
mality," Mr. Nevin said with a disgruntled pout, when

Broderick requested a private audience with Mrs. Addison. "The girl has already engaged herself to the fellow—refuses to marry anyone else—told us so. Gladys, er, Mrs. Addison . . . is worried that the child may be making a mesalliance," "But after taking a look at her young gentleman, I'm convinced it's a love match. What else could it be? Loren has nothing to commend him as a suitor—no fortune, no title, no address. The girl is clearly besotted."

Gordon instantly took umbrage, but catching Emily's twinkling eye and the cautious shake of her attractively coiffured head, he swallowed back the violent retort that had sprung so quickly to his lips. Still, he would not let his former ward go undefended.

"Broderick may not be up to the knocker," he admitted with a huff, "but he's got a good head on his shoulders, and he quite dotes on Rosemary. I think they will suit admirably," he said with conviction, "and I, for one, wish them happy!"

Mr. Nevin leaned forward, ready to point out still more of Broderick's obvious shortcomings, but as Rosemary entered the room at that moment, he reluctantly sank back in his own chair with a sigh. He would have to find fault with the prospective bridegroom at some later time.

But Gordon afforded the gentleman no further opportunity for such critical analysis. He began praising his former ward's virtues immediately and did not cease even when Broderick, accompanied by Gladys Addison, joined the others in the drawing room. Much to Broderick's profound embarrassment and Mr. Nevin's acute annoyance, Gordon continued his cataloguing of the prospective bridegroom's many fine qualities all though dinner.

"Can you not change the subject?" Broderick whispered to Rosemary, who was seated so conveniently to his right at the dining table.

"What? And appear to be less than besotted?" she asked with mock incredulity. A smile tugged at the corners of her lips. Rosemary found her friend's acute embarrassment amusing. With his flushed face and harried expression, Broderick was the portrait of discomfort—but a handsome portrait, nonetheless.

For a moment, she allowed herself to consider the plight of the vicar's daughter, who had a *tendre* for Broderick. The heiress put down her fork, glancing sidelong at her friend. He was blushing fiercely from the flattering tirade which Gordon had launched in his defense, and Rosemary wondered guiltily if their little charade would prevent Broderick and the smitten Miss Thatcher from making a match of it later on.

It was Emily Addison who finally interrupted Gordon's harangue. "Broderick is indeed a paragon of virtue and Rosemary an Incomparable! I wish them both happy." She raised her glass in a toast.

"To the handsome couple—a long and fruitful life!" Gordon added heartily.

Gladys Addison and Edgar Nevin murmured sincere but less enthusiastic wishes, while Rosemary and Broderick turned various shades of crimson and averted their eyes, more from shame than shyness. After the men had enjoyed their customary glass of port following dinner, they rejoined the ladies in the drawing room. Broderick, pleading a need for fresh air, quietly insisted that Rosemary accompany him. When Gladys nodded her approval, he grasped Rosemary by the elbow and led her masterfully to the terrace.

"Rosie, I can't bear this!" he confessed in anguished tones.

"Neither can dear Mr. Nevin. I thought I saw a murderous gleam in his eye when Uncle Gordon began to repeat the list of your uncommon virtues just now. It is fortunate that Gran forestalled him, for I believe my mother's beau may have struck Uncle Gordon with the poker!"

Broderick could not help but laugh. The long-suffering Mr. Nevin had endured as much discomfort as he had. "It is Gordon's affection that makes him go on so. But I cannot think what provoked the old gentleman to defend me so ambitiously in the first place," Broderick wondered aloud.

"I believe my future stepfather must have been finding fault with you."

"That may well be—it's something Gordon will not stand for—he is too fond," Broderick said with an appealing grin. Rosemary smiled back, but Broderick suddenly became more serious. "Really, Rosie, this is too bad! Gordon is delighted by this mock engagement and your grandmother quite beams with amused pleasure. Are you certain there is no other way to secure Lord Beverley's affections? I feel we have gone too far. Think how uncomfortable it will be for you when you cry off! Or will that be my responsibility?" he asked, unable to recall this minor detail in Rosemary's plan.

"Mine, certainly!" Rosemary said, thrusting out her chin. "Everyone would think you a shabby fellow indeed to cry off our engagement."

"Oh, of course—a gentleman wouldn't do such a thing."

"I, on the other hand, will merely be considered frivolous and fickle."

"And that will not bother you?"

Rosemary shrugged. "No, I don't think so."

"I've said it before, and I'll say it again, I don't like this one bit!"

"You must think of it as play-acting, Ricky. It's all a bit of fun, if you'll consider it so," she suggested with a wistful pout.

"If I had only myself to consider, I could do so readily enough," her fiancé said, "but I cannot like deceiving Gordon."

"Yes, there is *that*. I dislike being dishonest with Gran as well. Yet I must say, I'm surprised by her easy acceptance of the matter. I knew Mama wouldn't care, but I had expected Gran to be a bit more protesting."

"Perhaps she is aware of your scheme."

"She is not! She would hardly approve of it, and she would have said so."

"I am not so sure."

As the scowl on her friend's face became sterner, Rosemary frowned and said, "I am counting on you, Ricky. I need your help. I know that you do not relish the idea of deceiving Uncle Gordon, my mother and Gran, but when this is all over and done with, and I am Lady Beverley at last, I will confess the whole of it to each of them, privately. I'll tell them I coerced you into assisting me in the scheme."

"You did not coerce me!" Broderick protested.

"I bribed you then!"

"Neither bribery or coercion compelled me to assist you, Rosie!" he declared heatedly. "I'm helping you because . . . because . . . because I feel I *should.* Come to think of it though, I don't know *why* on earth I should feel so obliged. I must repeat . . . I want you to know, Rosie, that I cannot like this deception. Every time I see Gordon's beaming face, I feel rather sick."

Rosemary nodded glumly. "I know. He will be hurt more than any of the others, I think. I am convinced that Mama cares little for whom I marry as long as I *do* marry. And Gran simply wants me to be happy."

"Are you sure you will be happy with him—Beverley, I mean?" Broderick fixed his stare upon the moonlit garden.

"Yes," Rosemary replied with only the briefest hesitation.

"And will you tell him about this chuckle-headed idea of yours, once you are safely married to his lordship?"

Rosemary shook her golden head. "I don't think so. I doubt he would see the humor in it. Nor would he appreciate my efforts. I think it best that he remain ignorant of the entire affair."

"It's not right," Broderick insisted, turning his gaze from the garden to Rosemary's troubled face. "A man and wife should have no secrets between them. If you truly love him, you should be honest with him."

"You would preach to me of honesty?" Rosemary asked, with the lift of an eyebrow. Her eyes smarted, and she could feel the tears threatening to spill upon her cheeks.

Broderick stepped back, away from her. "If I am dishonest, it is for your sake, Rosie, and yours alone," he declared brusquely.

Stung by the truth of this admission, Rosemary moved toward him. She gently placed her hand upon his coat sleeve. "Ricky, I *am* sorry. I should have held my tongue. I realize that you have compromised yourself for my benefit, and I thank you with all my heart. You are right. It is dishonest all around, so I promise to make a clean breast of it—as soon as I am wed."

"Will you confess all to Beverley too?"

Rosemary hesitated. "Yes, as soon as I am certain of his love—I will."

"Rosie, I . . ." As Broderick placed his hands lightly

upon her shoulders, he pulled her closer and peered down into her face. He forgot what he had intended to say.

Stricken by his expression, one that she misconstrued as censorious, Rosemary put her hands against his chest and pushed away from his embrace. "Don't, Ricky, don't berate me," she implored. She hastily wiped the tears from her cheeks with the back of her hand. "Please don't make me feel more guilty than I already do. We must go in now looking like two contented lovers without a care in the world. We must!"

Broderick swallowed hard. He nodded. "At least we'll be leaving for London soon, and I will not have to look Gordon in the eye each day." He sighed heavily.

"Nor hear him sing your praises," Rosemary teased.

"That too," Broderick agreed, looking down at her with a crooked grin.

When they joined the others in the drawing room, they found Emily pouring tea, and Gordon praising not Broderick this time, but Rosemary. "She'll make a fine botanist's wife. When Broderick and I return to the Bahamas, she'll accompany us, and break hearts throughout the islands."

"Will I be going to the Bahamas with you, Uncle Gordon?" Rosemary asked lightly, entering the room upon Broderick's arm.

"Certainly! And to America as well!" Gordon declared, holding out a hand to her.

Rosemary slipped away from Broderick and joined the elderly gentleman upon the sofa. She clasped his gnarled hand between her own fair ones. "Why not Botany Bay?" she asked, with a coy glance in Broderick's direction.

"Why not indeed!" Gordon quipped. "We'll add it to the travel itinerary."

"I don't see why the girl should gad about the globe," Mr. Nevin objected. He turned his frowning countenance upon his betrothed, who sat rigidly next to him. Gladys blinked fiercely. Her hands fluttered in her lap. Not knowing what to say, she said nothing.

"A waste of money, if you ask me!" Mr. Nevin blustered on. "Young people need to settle down. Rosemary owns quite enough property hereabouts, and the young gentleman should make do with that."

A brief but uncomfortable silence followed this tactless remark. Rosemary glanced furtively in Broderick's direction. It hurt her to see the cold, remote expression on his face. He was not a fortune hunter, she knew. Any insinuation to the contrary would be extremely painful to her unworldly friend. She blushed warmly, but Gordon's face had turned a deep and dangerous shade of purple.

"Sir, may I remind you that Mr. Loren may wish to make *another* home for his young wife and by the gods, I intend to see that he can do it!" the outraged gentleman declared. Feeling the tremble of Rosemary's hands and fearing she might cry, Gordon was provoked even further.

"I intend to make Broderick a wealthy man!' he announced.

A barrage of excited remarks greeted this unexpected declaration.

"How extraordinary!" Rosemary's mother declared.

"What can you mean, sir?" Broderick demanded.

"Uncle Gordon, is it true?" Rosemary asked faintly, thinking only of Broderick's future happiness. She observed that Mr. Nevin said nothing at all. But his mouth opened and closed several times, like that of a fish.

"What of your nephew, Gordon? Is he not your heir?" Emily prompted.

"Oh, my plaguey nephew gets the Hall, of course, and the rest of my properties," Gordon admitted, with a dismissive wave of his hand. "But the money is my own. It came to me through my mother, and I will leave it where I will. I intend to bequeath it to Broderick. Why shouldn't I? After all, he's been like a son to me."

Noting the excited glow in Rosemary's eyes, Gordon placed his hand affectionately under her small chin. "Our Rosebud will soon discover that she has married a humble scholar with very expensive habits. I will see to it that he can well afford to indulge them!"

"Sir, I must protest!" Broderick began lamely, rising to his feet. His sunburned face was a mask of astonishment, confusion and guilt.

"You'll do no such thing!" Gordon snapped. "Sit down! I fully intend to make all the necessary arrangements once we get to London, and that's all we'll say upon the matter this evening."

"You're accompanying us to London?" Rosemary

asked hoarsely. She sat now on the edge of her seat. She dared not look in Broderick's direction for she was all too aware of how eager he was to escape Gordon's keen eye during the time of the great pretence.

"Of course I'm going with him to London!" Gordon told her, taken aback by her surprise. "Did you think I would not? I've already written to my cousin, Sir Stephen Merrimam, requesting that we put up with him. He's got a fine house in Grosvenor Square. Plenty of room. Besides, we can't have Broderick making a cake of himself. He needs a good tailor as well as a barber.

"Stephen will know just how to take you in hand, my boy," Gordon went on gaily, addressing the conscious-stricken Broderick. "My cousin is quite a swell! A pink of the ton! Yes, indeed! When he's done with you, Broderick, they'll all sit up and take notice of the Incomparable's affianced beau!"

Chapter Seven

"You can't say I didn't warn you, Tom!" Mr. Alfred Falkner said with grim satisfaction. He shoved a copy of *The Gazette* under his friend's aristocratic nose. "The beautiful Miss Addison didn't wait for you to come up to scratch. I said that she wouldn't. She's engaged to be married. Some chap named Loren. The announcement is in yesterday's paper."

Lord Beverley raked his slender fingers through his crisp black curls. His ice-blue eyes gleamed with unnatural brightness. "I know, Freddy, I know. Don't throw it at my head."

Observing his friend's disheveled appearance and his flushed cheeks, Falkner gave a snort. "No, I don't reckon your head can handle any further barrage. You're foxed!"

The earl slammed his fist upon a small table that seemed conveniently placed for such abuse. "Freddy, I don't believe it! I don't!"

"Don't believe it? Why, Tom, anyone can see that you've been drinking!"

Lord Beverley waved an impatient hand. "Of course, I'm foxed!" he snapped with ill temper. "It's Miss Addison's betrothal I cannot accept."

"You'll have to, old boy! Says so in *The Gazette*," Mr. Falkner went on sympathetically. "Mr. Broderick Loren is the happy gentleman. Never heard of him myself, but he's stolen the Incomparable from under your very nose just the same."

"*That's* what I find so hard to believe. I was certain Rosemary and I had an understanding."

"Apparently, Miss Addison did not understand well enough." Falkner pulled up a chair and regarded his handsome but discomposed friend with pity and impatience. "Did you ever mention marriage between you? You never mentioned it to me, if you did."

"No, but she made it perfectly clear that she would welcome my suit," Tom insisted. "I thought she understood that I intended to make her an offer . . . eventually." He rose to his feet and paced across the room. The bitter knowledge of Rosemary Addison's engagement was so palpable, it filled his mouth with distaste.

"*Eventually*," his friend repeated. "I told you that if you didn't make her an offer, some other chap would. Well, he has, and she's accepted. She could not wait forever, Tom. There's the matter of pride, after all. The girl is just as proud as you, Tom! You cannot have failed to notice that."

"Yes, she's proud, and that's why I find it hard to believe that she's accepted a rustic like this . . . this Mr. Loren. She was hanging out for a title—I was sure of it. Her mother, at least, gave me that impression. But this Loren fellow has no title, no lands, no fortune! How can Mrs. Addison have sanctioned the match at all?"

"According to the latest on dits, it's a love match."

"*That*, my dear Freddy, I refuse to believe!"

But if Lord Beverley found the heiress' engagement difficult to accept, he was in the minority. An entire host of anxious mothers with marriageable daughters of their own heaved a collective sigh of relief. They wished Rosemary Addison all the happiness in the world and were determined to welcome her intended into their midst with grateful civility.

The Honorable Clarissa Paige, Rosemary's closest friend, was pleasantly surprised by the news. A pretty girl with dark hair and eyes, and a gentle nature, Clarissa was one of the first to call upon Rosemary after her return to the city. "You positively glow with happiness, Rosemary, so there's no need for me to ask how you are!" The young lady bestowed a warm embrace.

"I am quite well, thank you!" Rosemary replied. Noting the look of curiosity upon Clarissa's eager face, she chuckled. "And I'm finally to be married! I will not become an old maid after all."

"Old maid, indeed!" Clarissa scolded, her eyes glowing with merriment. "As though you ever could! Why, it's only a surprise that you did not marry at the end of your first season."

Recalling the distinct humiliation of having not made a desirable match last year, Rosemary laid the blame at Lord Beverley's door. And since her return to London, he had neither sent a missive nor a bouquet wishing her happiness. There had been no indication whatsoever that his lordship was aware of her return or her engagement. Rosemary was convinced, however, that he *did* know and was too stunned—or angry—to respond appropriately. She hoped he was simmering with rage—no, seething!

"Come, Rosemary, I'm all impatience!" Clarissa declared with a nervous fidget. "Tell me! Is this young man of yours as handsome as Beau Brummel? As tall as Mr. Reginald Flukes? As dashing as Lord Beverley?"

Rosemary only smiled and allowed herself to briefly entertain the image of a balding Lord Beverley—totally bald, after having torn out his dark curls with hopelessness and despair when he heard of her impending nuptials to another man.

"You haven't even told me what he is like. Is he dark or fair?" Clarissa leaned closer, inviting the heiress' confidences. "Blue eyes or brown?"

"Wait and see!" Rosemary said with a coy smile. She knew her friend was expecting a lover's fond description of Broderick. How could she describe him so? Broderick *was* attractive. But was he handsome in a romantic way? He was taller than the earl and broader in the shoulders, but Lord Beverley had an air of elegance that Broderick did not possess. Besides, the earl's profile was very fine indeed. To Rosemary, besotted by infatuation, there was simply no comparison between the two men.

Clarissa would not be put off so easily. "I am certain that your Mr. Loren must be very handsome. All of London is saying that it must be so. A love match between two childhood friends. It's so romantic!" she gushed.

Rosemary shrugged aside this comment. "You must wait and see."

"When, pray tell, am I to meet him?"

"Why, tonight—if you attend the assembly at Almack's. Broderick is coming here for dinner, along with his benefactor Mr. Gordon Stanley-Hodge and Sir Stephen Merrimam. Then, we shall go to Almack's. Will you be there?

"I plan to be. Along with my mother and my brother."

"Then, you shall see me walk in upon his arm, Clarissa, and you may judge my dear Mr. Loren for yourself." Rosemary smiled at her friend and appeared to such radiant advantage that Clarissa gasped slightly.

"Oh, Rosemary! You must love your Mr. Loren a great deal," she sighed wistfully. "Indeed, I have never seen you in better looks or higher spirits. You are transformed!"

"You are too kind," Rosemary murmured, blushing deeply. Like Broderick, she was feeling the burden of this guilty charade. As she was silently contemplating this guilt, she remembered the promise she'd made to Broderick.

"My dear Clarissa, I would ask a favor of you. Ricky, I mean Broderick, is a botanist of some accomplishment, I can assure you, and he would very much like to meet your grandfather. Do you think you could arrange an introduction?" Rosemary asked hopefully.

"Why, I'm sure I can!" Clarissa replied, eager to please. "But with Grandpapa, one must be very subtle. If I tell him he has an admirer coming to tea, he may take to his bed with an imagined attack of the gout." Clarissa laughed, displaying small, even white teeth. "He's painfully shy, you see and doesn't go out into society any more—hasn't for years."

"So I've been told. That's why I took the liberty of asking you to arrange a meeting between the two. It would mean so much to Ricky—I cannot tell you." Rosemary clasped one of Clarissa's hands between her own. "Broderick is an enthusiastic admirer of your grandfather's work. The meeting would mean a great deal to him. It would mean a great deal to me as well to see him so indulged."

"Indeed, say no more!" Clarissa replied with a toss of her dark curls. "It will take some cunning but I shall arrange everything. Now tell me, is Mr. Loren witty?"

Rosemary laughed. "Did I not say you must wait and see?"

"Really, Rosemary!" Clarissa protested with raised

eyebrows. "I expected you to fall into raptures, to regale me with an endless list of your intended's many virtues. Instead, I find that you are mysteriously reticent. This is not like you."

"Hmmm . . . well, he is quite interested in exotic flora, as I've said, and he's considering naming an orchid after one of my lavender gloves," she announced proudly. "Rosemary's Glove! Isn't it a charming name for a flower?"

"Oh, your Mr. Loren *must* be a romantic, indeed!" Clarissa declared with a sigh. "And a nonpareil."

Even his most fervent admirers would not have called Broderick Loren a nonpareil. But under Sir Stephen's guidance, the young scholar was turned out to great advantage. He had come to town with Mr. Stanley-Hodge, and the two men had taken up temporary residence with Sir Stephen Merrimam, Gordon's "young cousin" who proved not so young at all, but a well-preserved three-and-fifty.

Sir Stephen, a quiet, elegantly dressed bachelor noted for his good taste and pleasing address, had considerable misgivings regarding the challenge of transforming his elder cousin's young protegee into a tulip of fashion. But after renewing his acquaintance with Broderick, whom he had not seen since the young man had left Oxford, Sir Stephen decided that the case was not as hopeless as he had feared.

Declaring that Broderick had fine teeth, an attractive smile, good legs and shoulders that would, fortunately, not need padding, Sir Stephen warmed to the task of turning the young man out in proper style. "Not such a Johnny Raw as you led me to expect, Cousin," he chastised Mr. Stanley-Hodge. Gordon, pleased with Stephen's assessment, only snorted.

"He's sadly brown, I'm afraid, and no amount of milk baths will lessen the burn he has acquired after years of scouring the countryside in your wake, collecting bugs and what-have-you," Sir Stephen announced. "Nevertheless, I am hopeful that he will turn out rather well after all."

The amiable Broderick, who gnashed his fine teeth in private and vowed he'd make Rosemary Addison finance *two* trips to Botany Bay in exchange for this agonizing ordeal, was taken to the best of tailors and fitted for an elegant but simple wardrobe. His thick hair was cut in the popular windswept fashion and, although Sir Stephen held out little hope, the young scholar was forced to endure any number of lukewarm milk baths in an attempt to lighten his bronzed skin.

"Damn me, Broderick, if you don't cut quite a dash!" Gordon declared with enthusiastic approval when he beheld Broderick's appearance that evening before dining with the Addisons.

Broderick colored with embarrassment. Secretly, he was glad that his appearance pleased his generous mentor. He hoped Rosemary would approve as well. The evening at Almack's was to be his first official introduction into society as Rosemary's fiancé, and while he did not care a fig for style and convention, he wouldn't for the world want to embarrass Rosemary.

Glancing at himself in the mirror, Broderick had to admit that he was not displeased with his transformation. However, he did not smile at his reflection. Nor did he respond to Gordon's enthusiastic sallies or Sir Stephen's calm assurances.

"Broderick, don't look so dismal," Sir Stephen chastised as he placed a reassuring hand upon young Loren's shoulder. "You are well turned out. I assure you that Miss Addison will be pleased."

Broderick nodded glumly. He was feeling rather miserable, if the truth be known, and he saw no way out of his present predicament. Gordon had kept his promise about seeing his lawyers and wrote a will leaving his monetary wealth to his protegee. An undeserving protegee, Broderick lamented. Then the announcement of his engagement to Miss Rosemary Addison had appeared in the society pages too. He knew all of London would be craning their necks out of joint to catch a glimpse of the green rustic that had won the hand of the dazzling heiress. Nervous tension and nagging guilt twisted his stomach in a dozen miserable knots.

"Stop worrying, boy. You look fine," Gordon hastened to reassure him. "You're bang up to the knocker. You may still be as dark as a gypsy, but I daresay the ladies will not fault you for that. Don't you agree, Stephen?"

Sir Stephen nodded. "The ladies will find him highly romantic," he said with a slight smile.

Broderick snorted. Romance! He never wanted to hear the word again! He had not enjoyed a good night's sleep since Rosemary had coaxed him into playing a part in her romantic scheme. Although sleep-deprived and guilt-ridden, he did not want to disgrace Rosemary in any way. His uncertainty made him all the more angry—with himself and his hopeless predicament. He just couldn't see how he and Rosemary could avoid hurting Gordon and embarrassing her mother.

When the Addisons' butler admitted the three antici-pated gentlemen later that evening, Broderick was hop-ing that he had successfully masked his anxiety behind an expression of bored indifference. Rosemary, how-ever, took one look at her friend's rigid face and her ten-der young heart was moved to compassion. She rushed forward to her ill–used friend and slipped a slender, white arm through his.

"Ricky, you are *too good*, and you look *so hand-some!*" she declared, breathless in her attempt to ease his discomfort. Her compliments were sincere. She could not recall having seen her friend in full evening dress, and she was mildly astonished at the transforma-tion in his appearance. Broderick was a man of ad-mirable proportions, she decided. His black evening coat and white waistcoat were faultlessly tailored, either by Weston or Stultz. She wasn't sure which. His pantaloons molded the muscles of his thighs. A single pearl was set modestly among the intricate folds of his neckcloth.

"You look quite princely!" she decided and meant it.

"A gypsy prince perhaps," Broderick responded modestly. He was greatly relieved that Rosemary found him acceptable and he felt a guilty pleasure by her affectionate attention. He knew she was just being polite and encouraging but he enjoyed the compliments all the same.

Gladys Addison wondered if Rosemary's enthusiastic greeting was perhaps unbecoming—even if the gentleman was her fiancé. She whispered as much to her mother-in-law. "I cannot say that I entirely approve of Rosemary's choice of a husband, but I'm convinced that *she* has no such misgivings. Indeed, it must be a love match after all."

"Indeed," Emily responded with a slow smile as she watched Rosemary and Broderick together.

"As Mr. Stanley-Hodge has left young Mr. Loren such a generous inheritance, even dear Edgar can find no fault with the arrangement now," Gladys went on.

"I should think not!" Emily felt that Mr. Edgar Nevin had little right to find fault with anything concerning her granddaughter's affairs. After all, the man was not Rosemary's stepfather *yet*!

"Tell him to smile, Rosebud," Gordon was saying. "Broderick's been acting as though he's going to a funeral." Before Rosemary could reply, he added, "But wait, if my memory serves me, an evening at Almack's *is* rather like a funeral after all."

Rosemary giggled and glanced up into Broderick's amused face. Her mother, shocked by Mr. Stanley-Hodge's unflattering comparison, voiced her protest.

"Really, sir! Almack's assemblies like a funeral? How *can* you say so?" Her eyes blinked several times in rapid succession.

"Quite easily, ma'am, as it is true!" Gordon frowned and continued with his tirade. "They serve nothing but lemonade and orgeat. The gambling is tame and the gossip vicious. And the harpies that call themselves the patronesses of those sacred halls—well, they're nothing but a bunch of old tabbies!"

It was fortunate for the assembled party that the butler announced dinner at that moment. Gladys Addison, her face a mask of astonished disapproval, recalled her duty as hostess and asked Sir Stephen, his lips twitching slightly, to lead her mother-in-law into the dining hall.

Broderick met Rosemary's merry gaze with one of his own. "Quite an enjoyable evening ahead, I perceive," he said quietly, his lips near her ear, as he led her into the dining room. "To think, I could be back in the peaceful confines of the country, puttering about in my greenhouse. But, instead, I've sacrificed all to attend the assembly at Almack's."

"Tcha!" Rosemary responded, with an elegant shrug.

"Count yourself blessed! Those not admitted through Almack's august portals are socially condemned. Why, even the Duke of Wellington was once turned away for not being appropriately attired," she told him with arched brows.

Broderick widened his eyes and assumed an air of feigned despair. "Begad!" he declared feelingly. "I am Daniel thrown to the lions. Is there no easier way for you to secure your beloved earl than to risk the lives of your friends?"

Two spots of color burned on Rosemary's cheeks. She felt so ashamed. The inequality of the situation had more than once impressed itself upon her. Broderick was the one making all the sacrifices, enduring all the inconveniences, while she herself had nothing to do but look forward to reaping the subsequent benefits.

"I appreciate your sacrifice more than you know, Ricky. You do not care for these arrangements, nor do I—not entirely. I will try to execute my plans as quickly as is seemly, I promise. Then you may go back to Hodge Hall with both your life and your conscience intact."

Broderick kept his gaze fixed straight ahead. He momentarily envisioned the hot-blooded Lord Beverley calling him out. A matter of honor. Pistols at dawn and all that. He would be fortunate to escape with his life intact he reflected grimly. His conscience had already been seriously scathed, so there was no hope there. And what of his heart? He'd been experiencing unfamiliar sensations associated with that particular organ of late, not to mention the thudding palpitations he felt now, being very much aware of Rosemary's slender arm entwined with his own.

His heart? Perhaps it was best not to consider that organ at all!

Chapter Eight

Rosemary was absolutely radiant as she entered the sacred halls of Almack's upon Broderick's arm. Her gown was a heavenly concoction of silver spangles and diaphanous petticoats. Her bright, honey-colored curls were arranged attractively. Her delicately molded lips were curled in an intriguing smile; her bewitching blue eyes glistened with excitement. Many a disappointed swain sighed with remorse. But there were twice as many ambitious mamas that fervently blessed the name of Mr. Broderick Loren for having had the good sense to secure Miss Addison's hand in marriage, thereby offering their own marriageable daughters opportunities to attract eligible suitors.

Glancing down at his beautiful companion, Broderick thought he had never seen a more dazzling vision. Who would have thought that little Rosie would become so . . . feminine? Broderick marveled.

Unmindful of Broderick's admiration, Rosemary glowed with triumph and self–satisfaction. She had dressed with extreme care and knew she was looking her best. Uncle Gordon had declared her to be "an admirable piece of perfection." She wanted Lord Beverley to think so too. Glancing casually around the room for any sign of Lord Beverley's elegant person, Rosemary felt certain that she could arouse his romantic intentions this evening.

"Is he here?" Broderick murmured in her ear.

"I don't believe so. Not yet," Rosemary whispered back. "But it is early yet."

He *would* come. She was certain of it. Lord Beverley would be curious to catch a glimpse of the young rustic that had captured Miss Addison's hand and heart—*and* her fortune. And Rosemary had let it be known to everyone she encountered that tonight she would appear for the first time in public with her betrothed.

Indeed, there were many at Almack's who had come for that very purpose—to satisfy their curiosity. Several gentlemen present had been so bold as to mention their keen desire to behold the "lucky devil." Likewise, there were ladies who entered those hallowed halls determined to make Mr. Broderick Loren's acquaintance—no matter how green he might prove to be. It was, after all, the very *least* they could do for one who had so cunningly swept Miss Addison off her feet and out of the marriage mart.

"Oh, there's my dear friend Clarissa—the granddaughter of Sir Halsey. Remember, I told you about her? How lovely she looks! I shall make you acquainted," she added, tugging at Broderick's arm. "Mama, Clarissa is here," she said over her shoulder, before sailing forth to greet her friend, who was suitably chaperoned by her mother and older brother.

Introductions were made all around. When Broderick turned aside to converse with another young gentlemen to whom Sir Stephen Merrimam took the opportunity of introducing, Clarissa gave Rosemary's arm a squeeze.

"Oh, Rosemary! He's so very handsome."

"Then you approve?"

"Need you ask?" Clarissa giggled. "He's so tall and romantic-looking."

"Rather like a gypsy prince?" Rosemary prompted, her lips twitching. She glanced at Broderick, who was conversing with Uncle Gordon, Reginald Flukes and several older gentlemen keen to learn of the adventurers' American travels.

Clarissa followed her gaze. "A gypsy prince, indeed." She sighed. "Or one of those dashing desert sheiks."

Rosemary smiled behind her fan. It would be no ill thing if all the young ladies carried away a romantic impression of her betrothed tonight. Such gossip, when he heard of it, would serve to enrage Lord Beverley all the more. And how Rosemary wanted to enrage him!

Moved by affection, Clarissa gave Rosemary an unexpected hug. "I like your Mr. Loren very much. I'm sure he'll prove to be a kind and good-natured bridegroom."

Rosemary was touched by her friend's heartfelt wishes for her happiness and only slightly guilt-ridden by the sudden image of a dejected Miss Thatcher, who had been wearing her heart on her sleeve for Broderick.

"Do you think he's as handsome as Beau Brummel?" Rosemary teased. She quickly swept aside all thoughts of the lovelorn vicar's daughter. She would not allow herself to think about that forlorn young woman in the countryside.

"Yes, and he has such a pleasant, easy manner. He would make his wife feel quite cherished," Clarissa added shyly.

"True," was all Rosemary could say to that unexpected assessment. Broderick *was* very good-natured. Glancing at him once more, she observed Broderick to be quite at ease with his rapt listeners. Rosemary hoped with all her guilty heart that her friend—such a dear, faithful friend—would make many happy acquaintances here in London. Perhaps there would even be a charming young lady who would capture his attention and his good, honest heart. When she eloped with Lord Beverley, Rick would then be free to pursue his own true love.

She stifled a sigh. While Clarissa was chattering giddily about Broderick's apparent virtues, Rosemary was thinking of the elusive earl. Where on earth was the man? He *still* had not put in an appearance. Where could he be? she reflected with mild consternation. If only he had more of the same good qualities that made Broderick so likeable, then it would be he and not Broderick Loren receiving felicitations this evening. But, no, Rosemary reflected with mild consternation, no, the handsome Thomas Alden was too proud. He'd played with her affections and refused to make an honorable marriage proposal promptly, when he should have. Well, she had her pride to consider too, Rosemary thought, a martial gleam in her eye. As she could not rely on him to make the first move, she'd been forced to use her own wit and cunning to secure her future happiness. In a way, she resented having to do so.

This thought gave her a spirited glow for the rest of the evening—a glow much admired by the gentlemen. Rosemary spent the rest of the evening dancing with one admirer after another, most of whom wished her well and expressed concern for their broken hearts. The militant gleam in her eye turned to a hopeful one when Mr. Alfred Falkner stepped up, asking her to be his partner for the cotillion. Mr. Falkner was Lord Beverley's greatest friend, she knew. Surely, the two had arrived together, she thought, her heart fluttering with excited anticipation.

"Miss Addison, please accept my earnest wishes for

your future happiness," Mr. Falkner said, leading her to the dance floor. Rosemary murmured her gratitude and glanced furtively around the room for a sign of Lord Beverley. A spot of color burned on each cheek.

"I'm sure had Tom been able to come this evening, he would wish you the same," the perceptive gentleman went on to say.

"You did not come together then?" Rosemary asked lightly.

"He worships at the feet of another goddess this evening," Falkner replied. Noting his partner's widened eyes and her sudden blush, he stammered hastily. "The goddess of chance, Miss Addison. Tom's at Watier's this evening. Again. He's had quite an extraordinary run of luck lately."

"Indeed!" Rosemary declared, and then could find nothing else to say at all. Following the dance, which seemed unending, she begged Mr. Falkner to take her to her grandmother. Finding that lady enjoying a comfortable chat with an elderly, hawk-nosed dowager, Rosemary entreated Mr. Falkner to leave her and took the seat on Emily Addison's other side. She waited impatiently for the hawk-nosed woman to take her tactful leave of them.

"What's the matter, child?" Emily inquired with mild concern as she turned to study Rosemary's face.

"I wish to leave. I have the most awful headache," Rosemary lied. "Where is Mama?" Her tone was waspish. She suddenly felt over-heated, irritable and out of sorts. How dare that conceited, penniless, heartless Thomas Alden go to his club to gamble when he could have been—*should have been*—here paying tribute to her, even fawning at her feet.

"I think the pain is located elsewhere," her grandmother threw in. "I suggest you stay to see this charade through."

Rosemary regarded her grandmother through narrowed eyes. "Whatever do you mean?" she asked, feigning innocence.

"You are playing a very deep game, Rosie, and I cannot approve—not now," Emily Addison declared. Her handsome face took on a stern expression.

"Why not?"

"Because I've grown very fond of Broderick. I always *did* like him. But he's gone out of his way to accommodate you in this foolish game of yours."

"And what game might that be?" Rosemary wondered just how much her grandmother had guessed.

"I can't say for certain, but you are up to something. I don't want to see Broderick hurt," she said bluntly.

Rosemary dismissed her grandparent's concern with a limp wave of her hand. "He won't get hurt. How can he? His affections are not engaged."

A quiver of distaste briefly contorted Emily Addison's countenance. "Have you considered Gordon's feelings in the matter? You cannot say that *his* affections are not engaged. He loves Broderick as a son and you like a daughter! Nothing has pleased him quite so much as your engagement to one another. Think how devastated he will be when you cry off! He will blame Broderick. Gordon, the old fool, believes *you* can do no wrong."

"Am I to marry then to please Uncle Gordon?" Rosemary asked crisply. "First my own mother rushes me into matrimony so that *she* might remarry and sail for India. And now," she went on angrily, "now I'm to take into consideration the feelings of a . . . a country neighbor!"

Her grandmother gasped with shock. "Keep your voice down, Rosemary!" she admonished, glancing cautiously around the room. "And keep a civil tongue in your head! Indeed, Rosemary, you must have the severest of headaches! I never thought I'd hear such unbecoming words out of your mouth! Gordon Stanley-Hodge has loved you for many years—as much as your own dear father did, I daresay. And Broderick—"

No, she would *not* tell Rosemary about Broderick. The girl was a silly, hare-brained chit or she'd have seen it for herself! In that moment, Emily was almost ashamed of her own granddaughter, and her disgust was all too apparent in her expression and demeanor. Seeing it, Rosemary felt ashamed and contrite.

"Oh, Gran-Gran!" Rosemary gulped, leaning forward to clutch Emily's gloved hands. "What am I to do? Lord Beverley didn't even come tonight! He's at Watier's. He'd rather gamble than dance with me! He's not even curious to meet Ricky . . . nor does he care enough to wish me happy." Rosemary moaned. "What am I to do? I'm so miserable!"

"You're a fool, Rosemary Addison!" Her outraged grandmother would have said more—she longed to give the child the tongue-lashing she deserved—but Broderick approached them.

"Are you feeling all right?" he inquired with a concerned frown. "I came to claim you for a dance, but perhaps you would prefer to remain with your grandmother? Shall I get you something to drink? And something for you Mrs. Addison?"

A warning glance from Emily compelled the young heiress to compose her dismal countenance and to present Broderick with a pleasant, if not heartfelt smile. "We've not danced together all evening, Ricky, I've been looking forward to it."

"I don't believe the two of you have ever danced together in all the years you've known one another," Emily put it. She smiled warmly at Broderick and gave Rosemary's arm a reassuring pat.

"I beg your pardon, ma'am," Broderick said, addressing her while holding out his hand to Rosemary. "But Rosie and I *have* danced together before. It was quite a romp, as I recall. She was nearly seven, and I was fifteen. Her governess played the pianoforte, and we twirled around the conservatory like two hurricanes in the tropics."

Rosemary laughed with delight at the recollection. Not a few heads turned in the couple's direction. Several envious young ladies thought privately that having a fiancé who could make one laugh with such joyful abandon would more than compensate for his lack of title and fortune.

"Oh, Ricky, I had completely forgotten that day! It was such a rainy afternoon, and you had come over in the downpour to humor me. As I recall, I was recovering from the chicken pox."

This time, it was Broderick's turn to laugh and Emily with him. He well remembered his little friend's spotted face—a face that was now turned up so enchantingly that he found himself wishing with all his heart that they were alone at Oakley or Hodge Hall. He led her to the dance floor and wished that they were anywhere far away from this frenzied crowd and far away from the shadow of Lord Beverley. Alone, he could take Rosemary in his arms, if he dared, and pull her close against his chest, where a treacherous ache had now painfully lodged itself. He would kiss her smooth forehead, her closed eyelids, her soft, blooming cheek with its bewitching beauty spot.

"All right, Rosie," he said then, wrenching his gaze from Rosemary's cheek. "Which of the fine gentlemen present is your accursed earl?"

He had some time ago given up trying to guess. Broderick was certain the man could not be one of the tulips of fashion. They had made such cakes of themselves, praising Rosemary's apparent charms—such hair, such lips, such a figure, and on and on it went! He hoped she was not expecting such attention from him—in his dubious role as temporary fiancé. After all, he was a scholar, not a blanc-mange poet! "Come, point him out to me."

"He isn't here." Rosemary sighed. "He did not come. I have quite demeaned myself, too, for I all but pulled the truth of his whereabouts from Mr. Falkner, his most particular friend," she added bitterly. "It appears that my accursed earl, as you call him, is gambling tonight— he's had a run of good luck. He won't be coming here this evening."

Broderick frowned. Rosemary, looking into his face, was reminded of a thundercloud. She did not guess how very angry he felt on her behalf. In fact, Broderick fumed. The man must be a veritable coward not to appear to wish Rosie happy, he decided. Broderick nearly voiced his uncharitable thoughts aloud. But one glance at Rosemary's upturned face, and the recollection of her unhappy expression as she sat talking with her grandmother and he decided against it. Her pain and disappointment was so evident that he could almost feel it himself. He forced himself to smile down at her, knowing that above all things Rosemary would not appreciate his pity.

"Well, my dearest, he can't avoid you for the remainder of the season, you know! Sooner or later, you two will have to meet. Perhaps the long separation will only serve to increase his . . . er . . . ardor," Broderick suggested, but without conviction.

Rosemary's blue eyes glowed hopefully. "Yes, perhaps so!" she said eagerly. "Oh, Broderick! What would I do without you?"

Jolted by the rush of affection that lit up Rosemary's face, Broderick became suddenly confused. His pulse began to race dangerously and he fell out of step with the music, treading awkwardly upon his partner's tender toes and his own.

"I beg your pardon," he murmured with deep consternation.

But Rosemary was too absorbed with hopeful thoughts to pay much attention to her friend's clumsiness. "You're right, of course. I daresay, you always are, Rick. Thomas and I *shall* meet sooner or later. He can't avoid me forever!"

Chapter Nine

After the ladies had been returned to their own residence following their evening at Almack's, Broderick was the first to climb back into the carriage, where he discovered that Rosemary had left one of her long gloves on the seat cushion. He smiled as he picked it up and carried it shyly to his lips. It smelled somewhat spicy, like a carnation—like Rosemary Addison herself. He tucked the forgotten article into his breast pocket as Gordon Stanley-Hodge and Sir Stephen climbed into the carriage after him.

Broderick fully intended to return the glove to its mistress at the next opportune moment. But the next few days passed in a blur of social activity, and as he watched Rosemary sink more deeply into despair by the prolonged absence of Lord Beverley, he discovered a mild comfort in holding the glove when he was alone. He realized it was a sentimental gesture, but lately, he'd begun to have very sentimental feelings about Rosemary and wished with all his heart they were back in the country—just the two of them—without all the social obligations. He admitted—but only to himself—that those had been the happiest weeks of his life. Rosie had dozens of pairs of gloves. Surely, she would not miss this one? He would keep it for himself, and when Rosemary was wed—oh, unhappy, miserable day!—to her elusive earl, Broderick would have the glove as a token to remind him of the weeks when Rosemary was his, even though the brief possession had been only a charade.

Much to his astonishment, Broderick found that he had made a favorable impression upon London Society. He was deluged with invitations. The men declared him a "good sort" and were well entertained by his tales of travel and his botanical exploits. The young ladies thought him excessively romantic-looking and the more mature ones found him to be pleasing, without being ingratiating. The mamas with marriageable daughters upon their hands thought him a godsend. His unexpected popularity left little time for Broderick to sit and ponder his growing despair. Besides, Gordon had presented him with a generous six hundred pounds with which to buy wedding clothes.

"Why, it's just a drop in the bucket compared to what Gladys Addison will spend on Rosie's trousseau!" the old man declared, when Broderick stammered a protest against such expensive frivolity.

The wedding date was set for the end of September, and Rosemary found herself reluctantly caught up in a whirlwind of shopping. Together with her mother and grandmother, she visited dozens of London warehouses and shops, where the young heiress was greeted with the excessive cordiality which her bank account inspired. Accessories were purchased and garments were ordered without stinting on cost or fashion.

"Really, Mama, there's no need for so much fuss," Rosemary protested feebly, while her dutiful parent escorted her tirelessly from one shop to another.

"The wedding gown should be of white satin, don't you think?" Gladys Addison queried her mother-in-law while ignoring Rosemary's protests.

"If that's what Rosemary wants," Emily replied.

Gladys ignored her, too occupied with making a list of further items to be purchased for her daughter's trousseau. At the same time, she made a mental list of those items which she wished to acquire before her own quiet marriage to Mr. Nevin. Her hands fluttered nervously in her lap.

"And Rosemary should wear a lace veil, don't you agree?" Gladys asked.

Emily simply grunted. Although Rosemary had not

confided in her, she suspected there might not be a wedding at all—at least not one with poor Broderick as the groom. Her granddaughter was harboring some guilty secret—that much she knew. She had concocted some plan down at Oakley—or maybe even before leaving for Oakley—and Emily wasn't sure if Broderick was aware of what was going on. He was a good-natured young man, and she hated to see him become the butt of Rosemary's joke, if that's what it was. Surely, he was not a part of Rosemary's scheme? Regardless, her disapproval of Rosemary's deceitfulness had caused a blight to mar the pleasure she had hoped to enjoy while shopping for wedding finery.

For her part, Rosemary's guilty conscience pained her more each day. Her scheme had not been successful thus far. She greatly feared it would not come off at all. What would become of her then? Should she confess the entire hare-brained plan to her grandmother and plead with that resourceful lady to extricate her from the web of deceit? With an anguished heart, Rosemary tried to dissuade her mother from carrying out any further excesses.

"Really, Mama, Broderick has no taste for excessive finery. He'd prefer a very simple ceremony." Rosemary's aghast parent quickly rebuked her.

"I care little for Broderick's preferences in the matter! This is your wedding, my dear, and I intend to see that everything is done properly and lavishly, as is befitting an Addison," her mother declared, her bosom swelling with righteous indignation. "Your dear departed father would expect nothing less."

"Rosemary, enough is enough!" the much-tried gentleman complained one morning while taking his betrothed for a canter in the park. It was the surest and safest place to talk alone, despite the many other riders who were out enjoying the air as well. "Gordon and Sir Stephen have ordered more clothes for me—more suitable for a king than a country-bred scholar. He even intends to send orders to the Hall to have a new greenhouse constructed at Oakley. Apparently, he and your mother have decided that you and I will take up residence there following the honeymoon."

The look of distaste on his face caused Rosemary to conclude that her friend considered the very idea of going through with a marriage to her repugnant. She was painfully stung.

"It took all of my cleverness to talk him out of the arrangement, let me assure you! I finally had to insist that *I* wished to oversee the construction myself."

Feeling waspish, Rosemary snapped back at him. "Oh, do be quiet, Ricky! You ramble on so that I cannot think! I had not expected this charade to go on so long. I cannot understand why Thomas keeps avoiding me. I've not seen him *anywhere* for weeks. Surely his anger must have abated by now!" Rosemary's face reflected the anguish so evident in her voice.

She had purposefully thrown herself into the gaiety of the season in hopes of encountering the elusive earl at some card party or rout, but she had not. The impatient heiress had attended horse races, balls, bridge parties and the theater, but she had not been afforded a single glimpse of Lord Beverley. She had begun to wonder if his lordship had left town. Rosemary made discreet inquiries to discover if this was indeed the case but learned, to her dismay, that the earl *was* in town, leading a full social life, which included an astonishing run of luck at cards. It was even rumored that if his luck continued, the impoverished earl might amass a small fortune—providing he did not lose it all at the gaming tables.

"I'm sorry, Ricky. I'm out of sorts and haven't been sleeping well."

"Nor I. We must put an end to this fiasco—*now!*"

"But, Ricky, I cannot think of calling off the wedding *now.* Not just yet, I mean . . ." Her voice trailed off mournfully.

Broderick snarled. He was growing more out of sorts with the unknown earl every day. It seemed peculiar that he had not yet made Beverley's acquaintance. The earl never seemed to be in the same place at the same time as either Broderick or Rosemary. Such elusive and suspicious behavior sorely tempted Broderick to plant him a facer the moment he made the rascal's acquaintance.

For the most part, the Addison household, which

should have been enjoying the gay frenzy of wedding preparations, was, instead, tiptoeing around Rosemary's sudden and unexpected weeping spells. Her grandmother, who normally delighted in the presence of young people in the house, made herself scarce whenever Broderick or Clarissa came to visit. Only Gladys did not seem to notice anything amiss. She was too preoccupied with wedding arrangements for her daughter as well as preparing for her own marriage and subsequent journey to India afterwards. It was the worthy Mr. Nevin who pointed out to her the change in Rosemary's appearance and in her behavior.

"The girl looks rather done in, don't you think?" Mr. Nevin had inquired one evening following a quiet dinner alone with his intended. "One day Rosemary seems pale and moody and on the next, she appears quite feverish. Is she well?"

Gladys only shrugged. "It is often so with a young girl before her marriage," she answered him with a knowing, unconcerned nod.

"Your mother-in-law is not quite herself either." Mr. Nevin refused to have his astute observations brushed off so lightly. "*She's* not getting married. What's *her* excuse?"

"She's writing a novel," Gladys reminded him, unruffled. "The process is not going as smoothly as she had anticipated." She regarded him thoughtfully. Her pursed lips twitched. Frankly, she thought her mother-in-law should be humored and said so. "The elderly should be indulged, don't you agree, Edgar dear?" she asked with a tilt of her head.

Mr. Nevin only grunted. He was still concerned about Rosemary. The girl was not looking at all well. And she had turned shrewish—a fault in any female, but particularly unbecoming in a very young woman.

Although Rosemary was indeed out of sorts much of the time, her friend Clarissa also put it down to premarital jitters. Entranced by Broderick's gracious charm, Clarissa dismissed her friend's moodiness as being of no consequence. How could it be when Rosemary was going to wed a man like Broderick Loren—so romantic, so kind, *so* attractive?

Under ordinary circumstances, Rosemary would have been delighted that Broderick should be the object of Clarissa's innocent admiration. In her heart, she guiltily acknowledged that a marriage with Clarissa would be just the thing to bring Ricky out of himself. It would improve his standing in society as well. Rosemary had also noted the admiring glances Broderick cast in Clarissa's direction. He always treated her with a particular kindness too, she'd noted, and couldn't help wondering if Ricky wished he was engaged to Clarissa.

It was an uncomfortable dilemma for the fretful heiress, and she could not see her way around the predicament. Nothing was turning out as she had planned—*nothing*. The early triumph she had experienced upon her return to London, secure in the knowledge that Lord Beverley would be properly astounded and inflamed by her engagement to Broderick, had withered into bitter chagrin. So, when Clarissa and her brother Harry suggested a picnic outing, followed by tea with Sir Halsey Paige, Rosemary accepted reluctantly but dutifully. She *had* promised Ricky an introduction to the notable recluse, and Clarissa, true to her word, had arranged everything.

The day of the excursion dawned bright, clear and pleasantly warm. Rosemary, having donned a becoming gown of yellow sprigged muslin and a large lemon-yellow hat with a white ribbon that tied beneath her chin, was escorted to the Paiges' barouche by her long-suffering childhood chum. Broderick, despite a manly effort, could not conceal his extreme pleasure and excitement at the forthcoming introduction to his scholarly idol. He was as excited as a schoolboy. Rosemary was touched by his uncustomary display of emotion. This was a special day for Broderick, and she was determined to be a pleasant companion so that he might enjoy the occasion to the fullest.

Broderick's enthusiastic discourse upon the work of Sir Halsey Paige enlivened their journey to the outskirts of the city. Harry and Clarissa, amused by their guest's boyish excitement, regaled him and Rosemary with tales of their grandfather's more adventurous botanical exploits. Rosemary smiled meekly now and then but remained silent as the barouche carried them to one of the natural beauty spots outside of London.

As Rosemary had expected, the alfresco meal was

lavish and carefully planned. Clarissa had thoughtfully seen to everything. There were thin slices of cold tongue, boiled eggs, small meat pies, fresh rolls generously slathered with sweet butter, a colorful array of cheese and fruit, a variety of pickles, cider, beer and for dessert, several dozen little cakes known as maids of honor. Harry and Broderick spoke animatedly of sailing, horses, and grouse hunting, while Clarissa, the radiant hostess, regarded them both with sparkling brown eyes and plied Rosemary with choice morsels from the bounty spread before them. The girl looked quite pretty in her white frock and a fetching hat with a bright cherry ribbon, Rosemary observed. When the two men excused themselves to walk off the temporary discomfort of the lavish meal, Clarissa leaned over and squeezed Rosemary's hand. The heiress couldn't help noticing the soft glow upon her friend's enchanting face—a glow that Rosemary had never noticed before. Fearing that she knew the cause for that radiance, Rosemary looked down at the tablecloth and studied it guiltily. Clarissa was in love with Broderick!

"Oh, you're so fortunate, Rosemary!" Clarissa declared. "But then, I'm sure you realize it. Mr. Loren is *so* charming. Even Lady Venerable said so when I went calling with Mama yesterday. We stopped in to pay our respects, and she declared that you had more good sense than she had given you credit for!" Clarissa informed her innocently.

"Oh?" was all Rosemary said in reply. Her color

heightened as she thought how unpleasant it was to be the subject of Lady Venerable's teatime conversation.

"That's high praise, indeed, coming from Eliza Venerable. You know how critical *she* is of every one and every thing," Clarissa chattered gaily. "She went on to say that she had feared you would marry 'that rogue Beverley'—those were her very words—and that you're much better off with Mr. Loren, whom she declared to be as sensible as he was charming."

"Indeed!" Rosemary responded in withering tones.

"Oh, yes!" Clarissa went on, unmindful of her friend's frosty glare. "And then Fanny, Lady Venerable's eldest daughter," she informed her friend unnecessarily, "Fanny sighed and declared Mr. Loren to be every bit as romantic as Beau Brummell, and her sister Marianne insisted that your betrothed was quite the most personable man she'd met all season!"

"How gratifying," Rosemary murmured. She smiled then, in spite of her annoyance. Broderick was personable. She'd always thought so, and she was pleased that Broderick had made such a favorable impression, particularly upon that stickler Lady Eliza Venerable and her equally censorious daughters. She glanced casually then in Broderick's direction. He was standing with Harry on the brink of the hill admiring the view. He wore pantaloons and highly polished Hessians that set off his fine, muscular legs to advantage. His snow-white cravat was intricately and artistically arranged. His appearance was elegant without being dandified. Rosemary observed with a strange, clutching twist of her heart, that Mr. Loren's profile was very attractive. Yes, Ricky, to say the least, was certainly personable. Marianne Venerable had declared him so. And who was she to argue with a Venerable?

Clarissa sighed wistfully. "He's had such adventures and is so knowledgeable about orchids and roses, without being tiresome. There's no other gentleman in London quite like your Mr. Loren."

"Tcha!" Rosie disclaimed. She decided that Clarissa had praised Broderick's charms quite long enough. It was high time that they changed the subject of conversation. "London is teeming with equally charming gentlemen, Clarissa."

"Perhaps," Clarissa replied doubtfully. "But then *you* did not find Mr. Loren in London. You accepted him while at Oakley! Perhaps I, too, should retire to the country for a while," she teased.

"There are more eligible suitors to choose from in London," Rosemary reminded her. "And I'm certain that you'll have an offer in the very near future."

"I *have* had an offer," her friend replied with a becoming blush. Clarissa lowered her dark-eyes demurely and pretended to trace the painted fruit on the plate that had once contained the eagerly consumed maids of honor.

Rosemary's blue eyes widened with surprise. She leaned forward and placed her gloved hand upon

Clarissa's. "Am I to wish you happy then?" she asked, breathless with anticipation. It would relieve her conscience considerably if Clarissa would accept an offer of marriage sooner than later. Her aching heart would be relieved as well.

"No, you may not," her friend replied, raising her eyes to meet Rosemary's own. "Harry and Mama both agreed that Lord Stavely could pay his addresses to me, but I have already convinced the gentleman that there is no hope in that direction."

After a moment's pause, she added, "There's so little to recommend him, to my way of thinking. All he's interested in is hunting. And he's so . . . so old!"

"Yes, he is rather," Rosemary agreed, releasing Clarissa's hand. Lord Stavely, had he heard this unkind assessment, would have been very much put out. For while it was true that he had a luxurious hunting lodge in the north and a notable stable, he was considered to be a well-made man and had not yet reached his fortieth birthday.

But it was evident to Rosemary that none of these material things mattered in the least to Clarissa. Guiltily, the heiress wondered again if her friend was nurturing a secret tendre for Broderick. The thought made Rosemary feel so uncomfortable that she found she could no longer sit still.

"Let's join the gentlemen," she suggested, scrambling to her feet. She offered a helping hand to Clarissa, and they then joined Broderick and Harry on the brink of the hill, where the two men were admiring a picturesque view of Elmhurst.

"Why, that's where Grandfather lives!" Clarissa declared with astonishment. "I didn't realize one could see the manor from this hill. How clever of you, Harry!"

Harry chuckled. Like Clarissa, Harry's eyes and hair were dark, his features pleasantly attractive. Rosemary had always liked Harry. She was glad that Broderick had struck up a particular friendship with him.

"I've been preparing Broderick for his meeting with Grandfather," Harry informed the ladies. "I didn't want him to be too disconcerted in the old gentleman's august presence."

"Is he a peppery sort then?" Rosemary queried. She slipped an arm through Broderick's, but fixed her candid gaze upon Harry's smiling face. She tried hard not to think of how comfortably pleasant it was to touch Ricky in such a possessive way.

"Don't worry, Rosie," Broderick said then, patting her hand and attracting her attention to himself. "I've had plenty of experience with peppery old gentlemen." His dark eyes looked down into her face with such a glint of mischief that Rosemary, recalling Uncle Gordon's fits of temper and brash manner, found her lips twitching with amusement.

"Peppery!" Harry exclaimed with some force. "My grandfather is anything *but* peppery. Why, he's so shy that he'd prefer to hold conversation with himself than to have to converse with anyone else."

"He's a lamb!" Clarissa declared, coming to her grandfather's defense.

"And yet, despite this painful shyness, Sir Halsey has kindly agreed to have us join him for a dish of tea?" Broderick asked.

Clarissa and Harry exchanged conspiratorial glances. "Well, actually, Grandfather doesn't know you're coming," Clarissa confessed.

"What?" Broderick declared. Rosemary looked startled as well. "Perhaps we should not stop by then. It's not quite the thing to catch him unaware. He may not even be at home," Broderick protested.

Rosemary could feel the hard muscles in his arm tighten. She sensed that he was bracing himself for disappointment, and her heart felt heavy. She suddenly resented the Paiges' deceptive scheme and longed to spare Ricky the acute disappointment, which seemed destined to follow the delightful picnic. Broderick had so been looking forward to this meeting. She could not bear to see his hopes dashed.

"Oh, Grandfather *is* expecting *us* for tea," Harry clarified hastily. "Me and Clarissa, that is. We thought it better not to tell him that we were bringing friends along, or he'd worry himself into a lather of nervous apprehension."

"Perhaps it would be best—" Rosemary began with, a disapproving frown.

"Don't fly into a pet, Miss Addison!" Harry interrupted. "Everything will be quite all right once we get there. My grandfather enjoys company when it's thrust upon him. It's just that he cannot cope with the anticipation of guests, that's all."

"Truly, this way is best," Clarissa insisted. She reached out a hand to squeeze Rosemary's arm reassuringly. "I daresay you and Mr. Loren will have a shocking disgust of our duplicity. Mama said that you might. But believe us, it could not have been arranged otherwise. You do understand, don't you? You will forgive our little deception?"

Broderick and Rosemary exchanged glances. He looked quickly away, murmuring something agreeable, while Rosemary smiled hesitantly and lowered her eyes. Who was she to find fault with Clarissa Paige when she had been telling one bald-faced lie after another?

"We shall bow to your superior judgment," Rosemary said then, looking up at Broderick to see if he agreed.

"If you're certain our unexpected visit will not be . . . er . . . of some harm to Sir Halsey," Broderick stipulated. "If he is in feeble health . . ."

"Fiddlesticks! Grandfather is as healthy as a horse!" Harry exclaimed. With that declaration, he turned back toward the picnic array, which was being hastily disassembled by the Paiges' two attending servants. "Your visit will be the highlight of my grandfather's week— of his entire month, I daresay. There's nothing wrong with him but accursed shyness. He'll warm to you in no time. When he realizes that we've brought a beautiful heiress and an accomplished botanist to call, he may never allow you to leave the premises."

The foursome made their way to the barouche. Rosemary chewed her lip with apprehension. It suddenly seemed very important that all should go well at the meeting between Sir Halsey Paige and Broderick. It was for this reason and this reason alone that her long-suffering friend had agreed to come to London masquerading as her fiancé. The meeting *must* be successful! It simply *had* to be! How else could she ever repay Ricky for his kindness? How could she, short of financing his voyage to Australia, reimburse him for all that he had endured thus far? Even that might not be enough, Rosemary fretted. What if Clarissa had fallen in love with him . . . and he with her?

Chapter Ten

Sir Halsey Paige was delighted to see his grandchildren. Their unexpected companions disconcerted him only briefly, for as soon as he had observed the undisguised admiration upon Broderick's face and took note of Rosemary's beauty, the elderly botanist, just as Clarissa had predicted, overcame his crippling shyness and made Miss Addison and Mr. Loren politely welcome.

Rosemary felt compelled to admit—but only to herself—that Sir Halsey hardly appeared to be the sort of individual to inspire unfailing devotion. The aging baronet was short, rotund, and as bald as a billiard ball. His complexion was scorched red by the sun and his attire, though neat, was undistinguished. But Broderick paid these no mind. He was simply delighted to have finally made the personal acquaintance of his idol. Sir Halsey was flattered by the young scholar's attention, and when he learned, through enthusiastic interjection on Harry's part, that Broderick was also one of the botanical brotherhood, the old gentleman turned pink with pleasure. He pressed Broderick for details of his recent voyage to America and the islands of the Caribbean. He then followed up the lively inquisition by offering to show Broderick and Rosemary his own greenhouse.

"I told you Grandfather would be delighted by your visit," Clarissa said, linking her arm through Rosemary's. The two young ladies strolled leisurely down the narrow aisles of the baronet's greenhouse, admiring the abundance of botanical specimens. "Despite his shyness, Grandfather has always had an appreciative eye for the fairest of our sex," Clarissa added with a mischievous wink. "Did you see the way his eyes lit up when he was introduced to you?"

"Tcha!" Rosemary declared with a dismissive wave of her free hand. "Your grandfather has barely taken notice of me, and that's just as well. I've not seen Broderick so elated since his arrival in London. I cannot tell you how I appreciate your willingness to arrange this meeting on his behalf," she added with heartfelt sincerity.

"It's been my pleasure." Clarissa smiled and glanced briefly at the three men before turning her attention to the nearest plant.

Rosemary, again feeling mild stirrings of guilt, watched as Sir Halsey proudly displayed his orchid collection. How she hoped she was not standing in the way of a budding romance! If only Lord Beverley would come to his senses! If only . . . but she immediately dismissed any further thoughts of Lord Beverley's unexplainable behaviour and focused her attention upon Broderick.

It was clear that her scholarly friend was in awe of Sir's Halsey's knowledge and his thriving display of the orchid's diversity. Noting the look of fascination upon Broderick's handsome features, Rosemary found herself wishing that he would regard her with equal admiration. This unexpected thought sent a mild but thrilling shock coursing through her veins. She could feel the color rushing to her face and neck. Broderick was so happy in his world of buds and blossoms that Rosemary envied him. Had it not been for her wanton plan, Broderick would now be working contentedly in his own greenhouse at Hodge Hall, planting and pruning the cuttings he'd brought back from his voyage. Once this charade had come to an end, Rosemary was fairly certain that she and Ricky would never be as comfortable in each other's company as they once had been. She feared their common guilt would not permit ease of sociability ever again, and she regretted it. She'd come to admire—no, more than admire—Broderick Loren. He was, in many ways, superior to Lord Beverley.

Wanting desperately to show her friend how much she appreciated his many sacrifices on her behalf, Rosemary gently pulled herself from Clarissa's affectionate grasp. She made her way to Broderick's side and quietly placed her hand upon his arm. But he was much too intent on arguing the finer points of the cymbidium over the cattleyas with Sir Halsey to notice her.

Rosemary squeezed his arm. "Ricky, does Sir Halsey have a bloom like the one you are going to name after my glove?"

"What?" the baronet said. "What's this? Has young Loren brought back an unidentified species?"

"I believe so, sir," Broderick admitted with becoming modesty, "but I cannot be certain." He proceeded to describe the orchid and where and how he'd come into possession of it.

"It's quite the same color as my lavender kid gloves, don't you know!" Rosemary interjected with a dazzling smile. "So Ricky has promised to name it 'Rosemary's Glove.'"

"If indeed I have the privilege of naming it at all," Broderick reminded her with a shy grin that touched the heiress' aching heart.

"How delightful!" Clarissa declared, her pretty face aglow. "To have a flower named after one's glove. It's so romantic!"

Harry laughed heartily. "Grandfather, you cannot be outdone by Mr. Loren here. My sister would have a rare flower named after her . . . er . . . after her slipper! You simply must procure an unidentified bloom."

Sir Halsey chuckled and beamed at them all in turn. His round, cherubic face glowed with pleasure. "I have had the opportunity to name a few flowers in my day. It is quite a thrill, I can assure you. But I confess that I did not know until today that young ladies could be so easily won over by such a scientific gesture."

"We would prize it above all things!" Clarissa insisted. "I would dearly love to have one of these pretty blooms named after my glove . . . or my slipper!"

"Or her reticule, or her Norwich shawl or even her hair ribbon," Harry teased.

The ridiculousness of his observation aroused their good humor, and before long the party was laughing heartily over one silly proposal after another. Clarissa declared that she never knew that naming botanical specimens could be so much fun.

"Perhaps Ricky and Sir Halsey will start a new fashion trend," Rosemary suggested with a smile.

Tea was served in a tastefully furnished room teeming with colorful examples of Sir Halsey's thriving plant collection. Because he'd been expecting his grandchildren, the baronet had ordered a lavish tea to be served in honor of their visit. There were freshly baked scones, bite-sized meat sandwiches, a variety of cakes and a lemon curd tart. Clarissa poured out. Rosemary found she had no appetite, and chose only a buttered scone to nibble with her tea. She told herself it was simply because Clarissa's picnic had been equally lavish. That, however, did not stop Broderick and Harry from consuming admirable quantities of everything upon the tea tray, while Sir Halsey beamed upon them hospitably.

Conversation soon turned to the acquisition of rare and costly plant specimens. "You actually pay someone to search the ends of the earth looking for plants for your collection?" Rosemary asked Sir Halsey.

The gentleman, a bright gleam in his eye, nodded vigorously. "Indeed I do, Miss Addison! I employ an intrepid fellow by the name of McCurdy. He's presently hunting in the jungles of South America, looking for rare orchid samples, for which I am willing to pay most handsomely. I wish I could go myself, but alas, we can't all be young and vigorous like your Mr. Loren," he added with an approving nod in Broderick's direction.

The words "your Mr. Loren" caused Rosemary's heart to hurt just a little.

"This McCurdy must be quite an adventurer," Harry commented. "Is that how he makes his living then, by supplying collectors such as yourself with exotic plants from faraway places?"

"Yes, and an ample living he makes too!" Sir Halsey added, passing his empty teacup to Clarissa to be refilled. "McCurdy is quite clever, and he's also careful. The man knows that he can get more money for the plants he collects if he brings them back without bruising them, and if the roots are intact."

"It's hard to imagine your fearless Mr. McCurdy trekking through the jungle, risking perils of all sorts, in his pursuit of plant specimens," Clarissa said. "One can imagine hunting for gold and gems and even costly animal pelts. But flowers? Think of it! Risking all the dangers for a simple bud."

"McCurdy's not the only procurer of rare plants," her grandfather told her. "There are dozens of men doing the same across all the continents, maybe even hundreds. But there are only a few who are masters, so to speak, and they all have their special travel preferences. I wanted McCurdy to journey to Botany Bay for me, but he's the self-proclaimed king of the Amazon, or so he claims, and no price would induce him to voyage to Australia."

"Broderick will be going to Australia after the London season," Rosemary spoke up without thinking.

Broderick fumbled with his teacup and regarded her with a hasty frown. Harry and Clarissa stared at her with open astonishment. Only Sir Halsey seemed to find nothing amiss about this unexpected revelation.

"How marvelous!" he declared with undisguised delight. He turned his full attention upon the slightly flushed Mr. Loren. "Perhaps I could induce you to collect a few plant specimens—"

"Grandfather, Miss Addison and Mr. Loren will wed in September," Clarissa interrupted. "No doubt the journey to Australia will be in the nature of a wedding trip. Isn't that right, Rosemary?"

Broderick and Rosemary exchanged quick, guilty glances. "Yes, of course, our honeymoon," Rosemary stammered. She gave Broderick a hesitant smile. "We've not yet told anyone . . . for fear my mother would worry."

"Of course, of course!" Sir Halsey interjected, with an understanding nod of his shiny bald head. "Still, if you *do* find the time, Mr. Loren, to scour the country-side—" He checked himself. Chuckling, he added, "No, I cannot ask it of you. It is to be your honeymoon, after all. Your mind, certainly, will not be upon collecting plant specimens. You will be traveling with an English Rose, which no doubt, will prove to be the rarest bloom of all."

He winked at Broderick and smiled admiringly at Rosemary, who blushed fiercely and resisted the urge to hide her flushed face inside her teacup.

"Thank you for a delightful tea, Grandfather," Clarissa spoke up. "But we do have a bit of a journey ahead of us, and we should be starting out."

"You promised to show me that sketch of the lavender phalaenopsis," Broderick reminded Sir Halsey. "From what you've told me, it may be the very orchid which I brought back with me, and have not been able to identify. I would very much like to see the sketch, if you and your brother can but wait a moment longer, Miss Paige," he added, turning to Clarissa with hopeful inquiry upon his face.

"Of course, they can wait!" Sir Halsey answered for his granddaughter. He pulled himself to his feet, offered his arm to Rosemary and said, "Let's find out about your orchid, Miss Addison. Shall we? Follow me, Mr. Loren. Coming, Harry? Clarissa?"

"No, you go on, Grandfather," Harry spoke up. "I've had enough flora for one day. I believe I'll go out to the stables and admire the fauna—your new litter of spaniel pups, to be exact."

"I'll come with you, Harry," Clarissa said. "Puppies, after all, are so much more amusing than orchids." She grinned at her grandfather.

"Blasphemous chit!" Sir Halsey declared with mock severity. "We shall join you at the carriage shortly. This will take but a moment."

He led Broderick and Rosemary across the hall to his library. There, he relinquished his hold upon Rosemary's arm and went in search of the particular notebook he had mentioned to Broderick.

"Ah, here it is!" he murmured, pulling it from the shelf. The baronet quickly leafed through the pages until he found the colored pencil sketch he sought. He offered it to Broderick for his perusal. "Is this your orchid?"

Broderick studied the sketch briefly. "It *does* rather look like it," he replied hesitantly. "Let me consult my notes, sir, to be certain." Reaching into the inner breast pocket of his coat, Broderick pulled forth a small leather-bound notebook that contained sketches of his own. As he retrieved the notebook from his pocket, another item, very much different in nature, fell to the floor. Flushing, Broderick stooped down quickly to retrieve the fallen article and restored it hastily to its original hiding place—the inside pocket over his heart.

The elderly baronet was too engrossed with the contents of his own notebook to pay any attention to Broderick's clumsiness. But Rosemary recognized it immediately. It was a woman's glove! She was always losing gloves and had several mismatched pairs, but had it been hers, surely Rick would have returned it to her by now. With a painful clutch of her heart, she wondered if the hastily recovered article belonged to Clarissa. She could almost feel the color drain from her face as she clasped her hands together to keep them from shaking. To whom did Broderick's treasured token belong? Was it indeed Clarissa? Or perhaps some other lady for whom he had formed a secret attachment?

Immediately distressed, Rosemary pressed a hand to her eyes and blinked back the tears that threatened to spill down her cheeks. If she had been feeling dismally out-of-sorts over Lord Beverley's unexplainable behavior, she now felt totally dejected. As the two men compared notebook sketches, Rosemary wandered over to the window and fought back the urge to sob. No wonder Ricky had been urging her to break their engagement! It was apparent that he had lost his heart to some fair damsel and could not declare himself. After all, he was engaged to Miss Rosemary Addison. No one in all of London knew the engagement was a pretense.

All thoughts and feelings, save those of profound guilt and misery, fled as she briefly contemplated the cruel injustice she had served her faithful friend. She did not, in that heart-wrenching moment, even consider Lord Beverley. The only thing that now weighed upon Rosemary's mind was the fact that she stood between Ricky and his future happiness.

"I'm so sorry, Miss Addison," Sir Halsey said, looking around for her. "I know that you will be sorely disappointed. But it does appear that Mr. Loren's mysterious orchid has a name already."

Rosemary only nodded. She could not yet trust herself to speak—she feared her voice would tremble. Nor did she glance up at Broderick as he came toward her and took possession of her hand, patting it sympathetically.

"Sorry, Rosie," he said, and she knew he meant it.

Determined to cheer her, Sir Halsey added that Broderick was certain to discover a rare specimen in Botany Bay, while the two enjoyed their honeymoon. "And I'm sure that what he finds there will be more deserving of the singular honor of being named after your glove."

The mere mention of *glove* pierced Rosemary's heart anew. If the kind old gentleman thought she was distraught over a silly flower, then it was best to let him think so. After all, how could she tell him that her intended husband was concealing a love token in a pocket near his heart and that it was quite possible that that dainty article belonged to Sir Halsey's own granddaughter?

Chapter Eleven

Desperate circumstances call for desperate measures, and Rosemary was desperate. The sooner she forced the elusive earl into a proposal of marriage, the sooner she could free Broderick from his gallant promise. In her anxiety, she never once considered how ludicrous her expectations were. Gentlemen rarely proposed marriage to young ladies already engaged. Beverley, although an impoverished rascal, was a gentleman. All Rosemary could think about was releasing Broderick from his obligation so he could pursue his true love—the mysterious owner of the cherished glove that he kept tucked away in a pocket next to his noble heart.

This thought caused Rosemary a small ache in her own. Forcing herself to ignore it, she opened the bandbox that one of the servants had just brought up to her room a short while ago. Rosemary admired the contents: A blue domino swathed in layers of crinkling tissue paper, along with a black velvet eye mask.

With a nimble step, she made her way to the long mirror to hold up the garment and admire her reflection. The hooded robe, made by one of London's most expensive dressmakers, was a most becoming shade of blue that brought out the sparkle in her eyes. As she was admiring her image in the mirror, she was startled by a dry cough.

"Charming, but you cannot possibly wear it. Your mother will never let you go to a masquerade at the Pantheon," her grandmother declared.

"Gran, I didn't hear you knock," Rosemary said with touch of reproach.

"I didn't." Emily made herself comfortable on the sateen–covered chaise. "You've thrown your money away, I'm afraid."

"I don't know what you mean," Rosemary said lightly, turning back to her agreeable reflection.

Her grandmother snorted. "That's a domino." She pointed to the garment Rosemary held under her chin. "An expensive one."

"I like expensive things." Rosemary shoved the garment in question back into bandbox. "Besides I can afford it." Then thrusting out her chin she added, "And I *will* wear it. It's a good shade for me. Broderick will declare me ravishing in it."

"Don't argue with me, Rosemary. You're not going

to the Pantheon, with or without Broderick. I will tell him it's not at all the thing—that you shouldn't be there, even under his protection. If he were not so green, you wouldn't have asked him to escort you there in the first place."

Rosemary's eyes blazed. "Ricky is *not* green!"

"Soft-hearted then. How else did you get him to come to London in the guise of your betrothed?"

"He's not soft-headed either." Rosemary ignored her grandmother's unsettling question. How much had she guessed? What did she know? "Broderick's kind and good-natured and . . . and noble."

"And green," Emily added with a curl of her lip. "He has no idea how deep is the hole you've dug for yourself . . . and for him. How is he to extricate himself without damaging his noble reputation? Did you think of that before you set your snare for your handsome fortune hunter?"

At that moment, the door opened a second time, and Gladys came in. "Who is a handsome fortune hunter?" she asked, looking first to her daughter and then her mother-in-law. "Not Broderick Loren, surely?"

"No, Broderick is a fine young man," Emily informed her. "Kind and good–natured and *noble*," she added, with a sidelong glance at Rosemary. "Your daughter should consider herself quite fortunate in her choice of husband."

Color rushed to Rosemary's cheeks but she said nothing.

"To be sure," her mother agreed. "Naturally, I wish he might have a title," she added with a short sigh, "but his birth *is* respectable and Gordon Stanley-Hodge *has* settled a generous annuity upon him. Rosemary is making a suitable if not splendid marriage."

"Just so," Emily declared, rising from the chaise. She made her way to the bed and pulled the crumbled domino from the bandbox. "But still, she will not be wearing *this* to a Pantheon masquerade."

"What is it?" Gladys asked. "A domino?" Her eyelids fluttered. She clutched her hands anxiously together.

"Yes, a domino," the elder Mrs. Addison affirmed. "And Rosemary thinks she'll wear it to the Pantheon."

"Oh, no, dear," Gladys said, addressing her daughter with a shake of her well-coifed head. "You'll do no such thing, Rosemary. The Pantheon is a vulgar place ... now. Or so I'm told," she added hastily, lest her daughter question the source of her knowledge. "Your grandmother is perfectly right. You must give up the frivolous notion."

"I will not!" Rosemary said hotly. She'd listened to the two older women with growing indignation. She simply *had* to attend the masquerade. She had heard— through a most reliable source—that Lord Beverley would be there tomorrow evening, and she intended to be there as well to use the opportunity to rouse his sluggish sensibilities. This, of course, she could not reveal to either her mother or her grandmother.

"As I'm engaged to be married, I cannot see what

harm can come of such an excursion—particularly as I'll be escorted by Broderick."

"In that case, I wonder . . ." Gladys hesitated, looking to Emily for guidance.

Emily frowned grimly at Rosemary's flushed face. "You are not married—yet," she pointed out. On a softer note, she chided, "Rosemary, don't be a goose."

"The masquerades are not at all the thing," her mother put it, following Emily's lead. "I am told that the people who attend them are quite low—that they use their masks and costumes to behave in a most disgraceful manner."

Exasperated, Rosemary snatched the domino from her grandmother's grasp and flung it on a chair. "Enough!" She sighed heavily. "I shall oblige the both of you in the matter. I will send word to Ricky that I've changed my mind. I won't go with him to the masquerade."

As the two ladies withdrew, Rosemary flung herself upon the bed with another loud sigh. Could nothing go smoothly? Must she meet with frustration at every turn? True to her word, she scribbled a note to Broderick, begging off from their planned outing on tomorrow's eve. But moments later, she wrote another note—this one to Mr. Stanley-Hodge, imploring him to assist her in a matter of some delicacy.

"Rosebud, what nonsense is this?" that gentleman asked the next evening, when he arrived to keep the designated appointment. He wore satin knee breeches and a black evening coat—providing a stark contrast to his halo of white hair. A black domino was flung over his arm and a half-mask dangled limply in one hand.

"You didn't tell anyone where we were going together, did you?" Rosemary asked, glancing at the black domino he'd brought with him.

"Didn't breathe a word. Had Stephen's valet fetch these things from the back of my nephew's wardrobe, but I didn't tell him what I planned to do with them."

Rosemary drew the hood of her new blue domino over her gold curls and smiled warmly at him. "Uncle Gordon, you're a pet to indulge me so. I thought it would be fun to enjoy a lark together—before I'm a dull, respectable married lady."

"But a masquerade?" Gordon asked doubtfully. "I think a play would be much more the thing, you know."

He had even more misgivings when they entered the ballroom of the Pantheon and witnessed the indecorous revelry already underway. "I'm too old for such nonsense," Gordon muttered.

Gleaming crystal chandeliers hung overhead. The musicians played on raised platforms, while droves of dancers swirled—and staggered—around the floor. Rosemary caught her breath as she took in the colorful scene. She tried not to ogle the notoriously painted women that successfully tempted passing men into dalliance. Broderick would have hated it. She was so glad now that she'd thought to ask Uncle Gordon to bring her instead.

Clutching his arm, she felt both trepidation and exhilaration. She craned her neck, looking for her quarry and absently fingered her own mask to be sure it was in place. She had not realized how difficult it was to recognize someone in costume.

"You don't expect me to dance in this crush, do you, Rosebud?" her escort complained, as they were jostled on all sides by throngs of costumed merrymakers.

"No, Uncle Gordon. Let's explore the salons and suites." Rosemary kept her eyes alert for any sign of Lord Beverley. "I want to see everything."

As Rosemary and Gordon inspected one noisy room after another, the heiress kept hoping for a glimpse of Beverley's elegant form. It was nearly an hour later that she spied him on the edge of the ballroom. He was dancing with a tall, willowy brunette in a rose-red domino. Her heart jolted. He was here after all!

She had no time to waste. Without considering the consequences, Rosemary let go of Gordon's arm. It was all too easy to become swept away in the swirling, noisy crowd. Although jostled about from all sides, Rosemary kept her eyes upon her chosen prey. She even had the presence of mind to bite her lower lip and pinch her cheeks in preparation for the inevitable encounter. The music stopped then, and Rosemary observed that the earl was leaving the floor with one arm clasped in a familiar fashion around his partner's trim waist. With her heart pounding, Rosemary increased her pace and hurtled toward Beverley like a cannon ball.

"I do beg your pardon," she mumbled, placing a hand on his broad chest in an attempt to steady herself. In stead of looking up into his face, she glanced over her shoulder in a nervous manner. She hoped the earl would presume that she was being pursued.

"It is *I* that should beg *your* pardon, fair Daphne," Beverley drawled, catching her by the elbows. "I am, after all, blocking your path. From whom are you fleeing in such breathless haste?"

Rosemary was aware of several different things all at once: That she was indeed breathless, that his hands were caressing her elbows in a most disturbing manner and that he'd lost his dancing partner and he did not seem to care a fig. Not knowing precisely what to say, Rosemary decided to say nothing at all. Instead, she fluttered her lashes and tried, in spite of her mask, to look demure.

"Your hand is trembling, Daphne dear," he said then, releasing her elbows in order to take possession of the gloved hand that still rested securely upon his shirt front. "Who are you running from? And why?" Beverley repeated.

"You have lost your partner, sir," Rosemary mumbled, taking another moment to look about cautiously. She was pleased to note that his gaze followed her own. He, too, was looking for her imaginary pursuer.

"I must not keep you from joining her—your lady," she said. Rosemary attempted to move away, and as she hoped, he prevented her from doing so.

"No matter. I have found another partner," Beverley said with a shrug.

Rosemary stepped back, trying to wriggle from his firm grasp. Her hood slipped back, revealing her mass of golden curls.

The masked earl gently tugged a lock of her hair, twirling it around his finger. "Hair of this color is a passion of mine," he confessed. Rosemary was hardly prepared for what he did next. Just as the music began again, Beverley maneuvered her skillfully and firmly across the floor to a secluded alcove.

"Sit down, Rosemary Addison," he ordered. "Tell me, what you are doing here?"

At the sound of her name, Rosemary flinched. "Do I know you, sir?" she asked with as much haughtiness in her tone as she could muster. In truth, she was more than a little startled by the masterful way in which he'd pulled her from the ballroom.

"Indeed, you know me and I know you," Beverley said, untying his own mask before removing hers.

"Lord Beverley!" she gasped. She fervently hoped she sounded as astonished she pretended to be. Thinking a tactical change was called for, Rosemary clutched his arm and heaved a gusty sigh. "Thank goodness! I *was* being pursued—by a very fat, horrid man in a crimson domino."

"In God's name, what are you doing here? Where is your escort? Surely your bumpkin of a fiancé did not bring you to this place?"

Stung by his insinuation, Rosemary thrust out her chin. "Mr. Stanley-Hodge accompanied me here—at my request. He's an old and dear family friend. Broderick's former guardian. Broderick Loren, my fiancé. I got separated from Uncle Gordon in the crush and then . . . then the fat man was impertinent, and I dashed across the ballroom to get away from him and . . . found you."

She sighed and cast him a grateful glance.

"Think you're safe with me now, do you?" Beverley said in a near whisper. His lips were dangerously close to her ear. His breath was warm on her cheek. He smelled of brandy. Too much brandy perhaps.

Oddly, without her mask, Rosemary felt vaguely exposed. She fretted, too, that Gordon was in a panic, wandering from suite to salon looking for her and worrying about her. In that moment, the earl gained possession of her hands and kissed her fingers, one by one. Rosemary felt faint from excitement.

"My dear Miss Addison—Rosemary—I had hardly dared hope for such a joyful opportunity," he said huskily. "Why? Why did you do it?"

"Do what?" she croaked hoarsely.

"Don't be coy," the earl rebuked her. He placed one hand on her shoulder and squeezed. Disconcerted, Rosemary was certain he was foxed. "You betrothed yourself to that Loren fellow!"

Rosemary gulped. "We've known each other since we were children," she answered lamely.

Beverley chuckled. "I'm sure your mama did not

approve. She was looking high, my girl. Don't tell me otherwise. She must have been as surprised as I was myself. But I daresay, you'll make the bumpkin a good wife."

"Ricky is not a bumpkin," Rosemary said hotly.

Beverley greeted this announcement with a humorless laugh. When he buried his nose in one of her scented curls, Rosemary began to have strong misgivings. This encounter was more difficult . . . and inappropriate . . . than she had imagined. She should have been dizzy with joy. Instead, she felt uncomfortably guilty.

"This is not fitting, my lord," she declared, her cheeks growing hot. She was, in fact, surprised to find that she meant it. And she was annoyed . . . with herself and Beverley. She rose quickly to her feet. "I am nothing to you but a temporary spell of madness," she flung at him.

Seizing her wrist, Beverly pulled her back to the settee. "Sit down, you minx! Don't tell me you did not guess my intentions. I surely guessed yours!" He laughed as he slipped a long arm around her waist.

Rosemary shivered as the earl placed a hand under her chin to turn her flushed face toward his own. "You *are* beautiful, Rosemary. Incredibly so," he said thickly. "You and your fortune will be wasted on that bumpkin. You don't love him, I know."

"I think you've had too much to drink, my lord," Rosemary said stiffly, turning her face away from his searching gaze.

"I *know* I've had too much to drink," Beverly replied with hollow laugh. "In fact, I'm foxed! I wonder, too, if I am a fool?"

Before Rosemary could respond to this suggestion, the earl pulled her roughly into his arms and kissed her—hard—upon the mouth.

Chapter Twelve

It was quite late when Rosemary finally awoke the following morning. She had a dull headache and her eyes felt sore and gritty. Her lips felt bruised from Lord Beverley's harsh kiss—or was it only her guilty imagination playing tricks, she wondered? The sharp ache in Rosemary's heart, however, was all too real. Only yesterday, she'd imagined the jubilation she was certain she'd feel if ever Lord Beverley held her in his arms and kissed her. Well, he had finally done so. Why then did she feel no joy or triumph? Where was the glow of satisfaction?

"Have I had any callers this morning?" Rosemary asked the maid, who brought her morning chocolate.

"No, miss, none that I know of."

"A note, perhaps, from . . . from anyone?" Rosemary pressed.

"I'll go see if the mail has come, miss," she said and left, closing the door quietly behind her.

Rosemary turned her face to the wall and blinked back the gush of hot tears. How could her carefully laid plans have gone so awry? Hadn't she dreamt of the earl taking her into his arms in a crushing embrace? Had she not longed for his kisses? So then why wasn't she pleased with herself this morning? Why was her stomach aquiver with dread and shame? She could only imagine what Lord Beverley must think of her wanton ways. She was engaged to one man and yet willing to kiss another. She'd been mad to conceive this foolish charade—quite mad. Whatever was she to do?

Rosemary blushed with shame as she recalled Lord Beverley's crushing embrace. Last night's romantic encounter had not been as thrilling as she had imagined or hoped it would be. In retrospect, she found it so distasteful that she quite understood why she'd fled the secluded alcove the moment Beverley had loosened his grip. With her pulse racing, she'd frantically searched the ballroom and two crowded suites before finally locating Uncle Gordon. She'd begged him to take her home at once. Irritably flustered by the boisterous masquerade, Gordon had been more than happy to take his leave, declaring the Pantheon a bedlam of madcap merrymakers.

In the hack, Rosemary had once again sworn him to secrecy. Gordon muttered something about "wits gone a' beggin" and "passing all bounds" but promised to not to say a word about where they'd been.

"You know, Rosebud, I don't think the ball was quite the thing, don't you know? I believe your mother would have disapproved—not to mention Emily, if they knew. Call me old-fashioned, but it's not quite the thing, if you ask me. Not proper at all."

"Yes, Uncle Gordon," she'd said meekly.

When safely at home once more, Rosemary bid her elderly escort good night and was more than a little relieved to learn that her mother and Mr. Nevin had not yet returned from the play and that her grandmother had retired early. Rosemary slipped quietly into her own room. As soon as her mother's maid had helped her undress, Rosemary flung herself onto the bed and cried herself into a troubled sleep.

Now, as she was trying to choke down the warm chocolate, she resisted the urge to cry again. As she wiped her eyes with the back of her hand, she heard a light tap at the door and sat up quickly, expectantly. Her grandmother entered, wearing a morning wrapper in a most becoming shade of plum. Rosemary leaned back with a sigh, the hopefulness slipping from her face.

"Who—or what—were you expecting, I wonder?" Emily said.

"Must you always be bursting into my room?" Rosemary snapped, as she tugged off her lacy nightcap and flung it to the foot of the bed. Her hair, she knew, was as mussed as her troubled thoughts. "Do go away, Gran, please."

"What *is* the matter now?" Emily asked, advancing into the room.

"I have a dreadful headache," Rosemary whined. She turned her face to the wall. A mist of hot tears rose to her eyes. "Please go away and leave me alone."

"I will not do either," Emily said, removing the tray and making herself comfortable on the edge of her granddaughter's bed. "I've had quite enough of your fits of temper and missish ways! You are not behaving at all like a young woman about to be wed. One day you are feverish with excitability. The next day, you are frowning and petulant. You should see yourself now! Sour-faced and ill-tempered. You've been crying—again. What is the matter? I'm not leaving until you tell me! And I have half a mind to shake you until your teeth rattle—then you'll talk!"

Rosemary, sniffing noisily, turned to face her grandmother's disapproving glare. Her first inclination was to say something waspish, but before a suitable retort could spring to mind, Rosemary's face crumpled. She flung herself into her grandmother's arms.

"Oh, Gran! I'm so miserable. I want to die!" she wailed.

"Come, Rosemary, it can't be all *that* bad." Emily gave her granddaughter a comforting pat or two on the back.

"It is! Oh, it *is*!"

"Tell me, what has happened?" Emily coaxed. "First, wipe your eyes." She gently pushed her granddaughter away and presented her with a clean handkerchief from the pocket of her morning gown. "Is it something to do with Broderick? Don't make me bully it out of you piece by piece."

Rosemary held the scented handkerchief to her mouth in a vain attempt to smother her choking sobs. Emily embraced her tenderly and said, "Don't cry, child. We'll set about making it right, but first, you must tell me everything."

Rosemary sat up more fully and wiped her streaming eyes. "I don't know *where* to start," she said with a gulp.

"From the beginning—that's always best."

So Rosemary began at the beginning. She told her grandmother everything, how she'd overheard Lord Beverley's unkind remarks to Mr. Falkner at the Bancrofts' ball. She confessed her scheme to make him jealous— and how she had cajoled Broderick into helping her implement the plan. Rosemary spared no detail. Blushing and stammering, she even confessed to last night's illicit excursion to the forbidden masquerade and the unpleasant encounter there with Lord Beverley.

"It was awful, Gran. He kissed me on the mouth and he smelled strongly of brandy," Rosemary complained, shuddering.

"Foxed, was he? That explains his behavior, but certainly not yours."

"Don't be cross," Rosemary implored with a ragged sigh.

"Are you certain you've told me everything?"

Rosemary sniffed once or twice while carefully considering her grandmother's question. She could not tell anyone about the token Broderick kept in a pocket next to his heart. Nor would she share the quiet but growing despair she felt whenever she considered that cherished item. She simply couldn't. Nor could she tell her grandmother how she glowed inside each time Rick looked at her and smiled or how her heart raced a little each time he walked into the room. It was all so confusing—and unexpected. Nothing had turned out as she'd planned.

"Yes, that's everything," Rosemary lied.

At first, her grandmother said nothing. She merely sat in silence, regarding her granddaughter thoughtfully, while Rosemary plucked nervously at one of the lace–trimmed pillows.

"Rosemary, you must have taken temporary leave of your senses. I assure you that I feel ill-used. I was the one who convinced your mother that you needed a repairing lease and that we should make haste to Oakley. If I had had any idea that you could be so foolish, I would not have consented to go. Nor would I have consented to this mock engagement. I pity Broderick!" she said with feeling. "You have been a poor friend to him, my dear. A poor friend, indeed. What were you thinking?"

"Don't scold, Gran," Rosemary implored with a watery sniff. "I already feel horrid. Please, help me undo this odious scheme. I don't know what to do. I'm at my wit's end. Nothing is as it should be, as I thought *it would* be. You must help me find a way to end this charade."

"Yes, I will help you," Emily assured her. "I feel it is my duty. At the time, I wondered if you were contemplating some mischief. But how you conceived such an abominable plan—and convinced young Loren to play along—I cannot imagine. I shudder to think what your mother will say about this."

"Must we tell her?" Rosemary croaked with dismay. She sat up in the bed with a jerk and took a swipe at her eyes. "Can't we manage—just the two of us—to set things right? The charade has all been for nothing. I don't want to marry Lord Beverley."

"Did he ask you?" Her grandmother arched an eyebrow.

"No." Heaving a sigh, Rosemary closed her eyes and said, "We must call off the wedding at once. Mama will be shocked and dismayed."

"Shocked and dismayed," Emily repeated. "What about the wedding dress and the bridal supper? The trousseau? It's all been a shocking waste of effort and money. And that is not to mention the preparations Gladys is making for her own wedding to Mr. Nevin and their subsequent voyage to India. Naturally, those arrangements will have to be postponed. I hardly see how we can call off your engagement without telling your poor mother. And what about Broderick?"

"What about him?" Rosemary replied, chewing on her lower lip.

"Think, my dear girl! You cajoled him into playing the key role in this charade. We must give him a new part to play, and I don't want him cast in the role of the villain. You will appear merely young and fickle when you cry off, but Broderick will be suspect. I want to minimize that as much as possible."

"I suppose you're right," Rosemary said, twisting her grandmother's limp handkerchief into a lumpy knot.

"Of course I'm right! But you must not speak to Broderick about the matter—not yet. I cannot trust you not to make a muddle of it—again." She rose from the bed and began pacing to and fro in front of the window. "You'll have to tell Gordon the truth—or had you planned to let Broderick bear that responsibility?"

"Perhaps we should tell Uncle Gordon last of all?"

"Yes, he will certainly take it badly. I do hope Gordon won't renege on his financial commitments to Broderick. Heaven knows, the poor boy has earned the money—putting up with *your* madcap scheme all these many weeks. I'm sure I feel sorry for them both. Here they are twiddling their thumbs in London, when they could be in the country happily absorbed with their bugs and buds."

Rosemary's lip quivered, but before she could indulge in another fit of tears, Emily distracted her by standing beside the bed and asking rather forcefully, "Am I correct in assuming that you no longer care to receive an offer of marriage from Lord Beverley?"

"No, I do not wish to marry him," Rosemary said, shuddering with distaste.

"Whatever made you think he would offer marriage *after* you'd betrothed yourself to Broderick? I cannot imagine it! What a goose you are!" Emily began her pacing anew. "However, once you break your engagement to Broderick, I have no doubt whatsoever that Beverley will propose to you."

"How could I have been so wrong about him? I thought him so handsome, so amiable. Last year, when he did not offer for me at the end of the season, I was so very disappointed—and hurt."

"No, he didn't hurt you, Rosemary, he merely injured your pride. Had you truly loved him, you would not have conjured such a trick as this one. And had he truly loved you, there would have been no need for you to do so, for he would have made you an offer at the end of last year's season. I quite understand how you could presume that he would offer for you, but Beverley has often confounded expectation. I grant you, he's a handsome rouge, but you would not suit."

"I think you are right."

"I *know* I am right," her grandmother said, seating herself in the chair at the dressing table. "You and Beverley both suffer from excessive pride. It's one of the seven deadly sins, you know."

"What . . . what shall we do about *him*? I never want to set eyes upon him again. I could not . . . I dare not."

Her grandmother snorted. "Leave him to me! He has

behaved in a most unseemly manner, and I will tell him so. And listen to me, my good girl, you will not shrink from him should you meet at the assemblies or in the park or at a party. You will remember that you are an Addison and act accordingly."

"I will try," Rosemary promised meekly.

"You must. You cannot hope to avoid him forever. You will not simper and faint or do anything so missish. You will stay close to Broderick's side, or mine, or your mother's when we are in public. You will be excessively polite, nothing more."

"I *will* try," Rosemary said with more resolve.

"For your sake as well as Broderick's."

Rosemary frowned. "Why for Ricky's sake? What does it have to do with him?"

"Broderick is your fiancé—or so all of London believes. You will see this through without shaming him or yourself." Her tone afforded no dissent. "Did anyone see Beverley kiss you?"

Rosemary shook her head. "We were alone in a secluded alcove. There were curtains. It was dark."

"And you told no one about the incident? Not even Gordon?"

"I've only confided in you, Gran."

"Then you must not tell anyone—not even Clarissa. The fewer who know about the unfortunate incident, the better."

"I won't tell a soul. I am too ashamed."

"Good girl. Of course, the easiest course to pursue

would be to go ahead with your wedding to Broderick Loren," she went on, studying Rosemary with a side-long glance. "I've grown quite fond of him, you know. He has a sensible head on his shoulders, and I believe he would make you a good husband. He's fond of you too."

"It is . . . not possible," Rosemary answered in a near whisper. She focused her attention on a speck of lint on the pink bed coverlet.

"Hmmm," was all her grandmother said to that. After a moment, Emily asked, "There's no hope in that direction? None at all? Could you not . . . ?"

"No," Rosemary answered hoarsely.

"Surely, his affections are not engaged elsewhere?"

"I don't know. He does not—would not—talk of such things to me."

Emily, regarding her thoughtfully, answered with a vague, "Hmmm."

"It's all such a muddle," Rosemary said with a hic-cup. "And it's all my fault."

"Yes—on both counts. Promise me that you will not do or say anything about this matter until I have de-cided how to handle the situation. No more schemes, no conspiracies. Give me your promise."

Rosemary nodded and reached for her grandmother's hands. She squeezed them between her own and gave her a grateful smile. "Oh, Gran! I *am* a goose."

"Yes, you are," Emily replied, but not unkindly.

"What was I thinking?"

"You were *not* thinking at all! That's the root of the problem."

When Rosemary's lip began to quiver once more, Emily moved over to the bed and embraced her granddaughter tenderly. "No more tears, Rosemary. We will see this through together. It will come out right in the end, I promise. Now, get dressed and come downstairs for luncheon. A little cold chicken and a glass of wine will bring the roses back to your cheeks."

As Rosemary kissed her grandmother on the cheek, there was a knock at the door. The maid came in carrying a large basket of mixed flowers in a rainbow of colors.

"I brought it up straight away, miss," she declared, breathless from her ascent up the stairs. "There's a note."

Emily, perusing the flowers disdainfully, plucked the note from the bouquet and handed it to Rosemary. "Red carnations and red tulips, primrose, zinnia, pink roses and baby's breath." She frowned. "Do you know what it means, in the language of flowers?"

When Rosemary shook her head, Emily interpreted the sender's secret message and indicated the various flowers one by one: "*My heart aches for you. I cannot live without you. My love is true,* and so on and so forth."

"You can guess who sent them," Rosemary said, extending the note for her grandmother's perusal. It was signed simply "Beverley."

Emily snorted.

"Where shall I put them, miss?" the maid asked, looking around for a suitable place.

Rosemary sighed. She'd been both hoping for and dreading some missive from Lord Beverley. Now that it had arrived, it seemed anticlimactic. She had to buck up. She was an Addison after all. Glancing at her grandmother, Rosemary noted the look of skeptical inquiry on Emily's face. She gave her grandmother a slow, mischievous smile.

"Take them to the kitchen," she said decisively. "Take them downstairs to the cook, with my compliments, and tell her she may do what she will with them."

"Below stairs, miss?" the maid asked uncertainly, her eyebrows arched in disbelief. "These fine flowers?"

"Yes, take them away to the kitchen," Emily repeated, before Rosemary could change her mind. She made her way to the door, holding it wide so that the bemused maid could pass through more easily. A young footman stood in the hall. He exchanged a few words with the maid as she passed with the heavy floral arrangement. Emily smiled slightly when she overheard the muttered words "off her nut." She turned when Rosemary spoke.

"I feel so much better!" Rosemary declared, as she flung back the covers and lowered her bare feet to the floor. "I do believe the dark clouds are lifting."

"Good," Emily said. "Perhaps you will permit yourself to enjoy the watercolor exhibit this afternoon. You do remember that we'd planned on going today with Broderick and Gordon?"

"I remember, and I'm determined to enjoy myself. But what are you going to do about my . . . my predicament, Gran? Do you have a plan in mind?"

"Not yet. It's rather like plotting a novel, don't you know? However, I intend to give it my best creative effort."

"I hope it will have a happy ending," Rosemary said wistfully.

Emily gave Rosemary a fond embrace. "Yes, it will have a happy ending and a surprise twist or two along the way."

Chapter Thirteen

"I had hoped to find a good face or two, but I see that there are mainly landscapes and flower arrangements and odd collections of inanimate objects," Emily lamented as she scanned the numerous paintings on the wall.

"There's an exhibit of portrait artists at the British Gallery for that, Mrs. Addison," Broderick informed her. "The paintings will be on display through the end of the month, I believe."

"What do you consider a 'good face' and what do you want with one?" Gordon Stanley-Hodge asked.

"For one of the characters in my novel," Emily replied. "I cannot envision Hippolyta and had hoped to find a face that suits her temperament. It will bring her to life in my imagination."

Gordon snorted. "Romantic fiction!"

"Hippolyta?" Rosemary chuckled. "What kind of name is that for a heroine of a romance novel?"

"Hippolyta is a heroine of Greek mythology," Broderick explained. "She was a queen of the Amazons."

"But my Hippolyta is a villainess—a mean and spiteful wench," Emily said with a smile over her shoulder.

"Do not tell me you are *still* working on that same manuscript—the one you kept scribbling on down at Oakley?" Gordon exclaimed.

"Yes, the same," Emily answered coldly.

"A colossal waste of time, if you ask me," Gordon declared, running a hand through his thatch of snow-white hair.

"No one asked you," she snapped back, her eyes dark with indignation. "Writing a novel is no more a waste of time than pinning bugs to length of velvet!"

Sensing that a vigorous argument was about to ensue, Broderick clasped Rosemary by the elbow and led her away into an adjoining gallery. She followed him willingly.

"Dahlias, chrysanthemums, water lilies," he said, identifying the flowers in three paintings before them. "Which do you prefer, Rosie?"

Rosemary blushed slightly as she recalled the colorful bouquet from Lord Beverley that had arrived for her earlier. Glancing at the paintings on the wall, she said softly, "I prefer orchids."

Broderick laughed. His eyes crinkled at the corners.

"What discerning taste you have! We shall have to search one out for you."

"Are not orchids your favorite too?" Rosemary asked, allowing him to lead her from one exhibit to the next. She was determined to enjoy herself. She'd promised her grandmother she would.

"They fascinate me, certainly. Gordon and I went to Kew Gardens to see the collection there—less than 50 specimens. I have more than that in my own collection. Sir Stephen thinks I should address the Royal Horticultural Society and bring some of my prized specimens for display. Did I tell you that at Kew there is a rare orchid with the scent of warm chocolate?"

"Really?"

"Yes, and there's another that gives off the odor of rotting meat."

"Astonishing!" Rosemary fixed her gaze upon Broderick's handsome face and wondered why he could make the most ordinary topics so interesting.

"And while orchids are still curiosities here, they have been collectors' prized specimens in China for hundreds of year," Broderick went on, enthused. "During the Ming Dynasty, orchids were used for medicinal purposes to treat all manner of ailments—boils, neuralgia, headaches, ptomaine poisoning from bad fish."

Rosemary was certain that Lord Beverley didn't know half as much as Broderick did. "Ricky, you *should* give a lecture. You know so many interesting things about orchids and other flowers too. They'd love to know about the ones you brought back from America."

Broderick shot her a glance and asked, "Why are we discussing orchids when we have a moment to ourselves—alone? How goes it with your elusive earl? I do not understand why I have yet to meet the man. It's been weeks. I was beginning to think he is a figment of your imagination."

"He is all too real," Rosemary said, lowering her eyes to the floor.

"I know that he is. I met a man by the name of Falkner. Seems to be a particular friend of the mysterious Lord Beverley."

"Mr. Alfred Falkner. Blond hair, weak chin." Rosemary paused in front of a canvas with bold red poppies.

"Yes, the same," Broderick said. After a brief silence, he said, "I'm vexed with you, Rosemary. When you regaled me with the list of your beloved's virtues, you failed to tell me that he has more creditors than one can shake a stick at. He has absolutely no notion of economy."

"I told you he was in debt. I believe I even called him a fortune hunter."

"Yes, you did," he admitted. "But I've since wondered many times since why you're so besotted. I've come to believe he's not a man of upright principles, and I don't know why you would hold such a man in high esteem. He has gaming debts. His estates are impoverished."

"Mr. Falkner told you all this?" She was incredulous. Although she well knew about the earl's debts, she didn't believe one's best friend should discuss them so freely with others.

"No, Mr. Falkner told me that Beverley was having a great run of luck at the gaming tables and that he'd been considering asking for your hand in marriage before I cut him out." He paused, waiting for her reaction to this announcement.

"Indeed," was all she said, keeping her eyes fixed on the painted poppies.

"Why the devil didn't you tell me he was such a ramshackle character? Others have mentioned him in conversation and most agree that he's dashing and charming and warmhearted to his friends. Others say Beverley is always ripe for a spree. Unsettled and irresponsible. I've also heard . . . other things."

"What sort of things?" Rosemary asked, knowing all too well what those might be.

"Things that convince me he'd be a most unsuitable husband for you, Rosie." There was a long pause. When he could stand the silence no longer, Broderick added, "I briefly considered seeking the man out and having a word with him—in private."

"Broderick!" Rosemary exclaimed, aghast. "You would not? You must not! You wouldn't do anything so vulgar, would you?" She clutched his arm and turned large stricken eyes upon him.

"Calm yourself, Rosie. I said I had briefly

considered—and that only. It didn't take me long to realize that *that* idea was every bit as chuckle–headed as your original scheme. What would I say to him in such circumstances? 'Your lordship, my affianced wife, Miss Rosemary Addison, is engaged to me for the sole purpose of making you jealous.' " He gave a short, humorless laugh. "Marry him, Rosie, and you'll quickly regret your imprudence."

Rosemary suddenly felt wobbly kneed. She feared she would swoon.

"What is the matter?" Broderick demanded. He took her firmly by the elbow and led her to the nearest chair, urging her to be seated.

Rosemary pasted a smile on her face and said, "I'm all right. Just a little lightheaded." Desiring a change of subject, she asked, "Are you tired of London, Rick? Do you miss your greenhouse and the vicar's daughter? Miss Thatcher, isn't it?" She'd wondered on the carriage ride to the exhibit if the love token—the glove— perhaps belonged to the vicar's daughter.

"Good gracious," Broderick muttered as he rolled his eyes.

Rosemary smiled up at him and squeezed his hand. "I should not tease you so. I *am* sorry. You have been too good a friend. I *know* you do not care for Miss Thatcher." At least she hoped not.

"Not a fig," he confessed.

"And you must be tired of town by now. The endless whist parties and dances and assemblies. You are used to a more studious life and you must be longing for your books and blooms."

"I confess I do miss my quiet pursuits. I wish I'd brought the new microscope, but Gordon insisted there would be little time for such pleasures. He was right. And Sir Stephen has insisted on hosting tonight's party at Vauxhall Gardens simply because I've never been."

"You will like the Gardens, Ricky," Rosemary assured him. "There are water cascades and fireworks and lots of flowers."

Broderick shrugged impatiently. "I'm not looking forward to it. It's one more frivolity, that is all. You are the only one that makes these outings at all tolerable, Rosie. You are a very agreeable companion."

He blushed when he said it. Rosemary blushed too, with genuine pleasure. "What a kind thing to say, Ricky. Thank you."

She rose from the chair then and allowed him to lead her to another quartet of paintings—roses this time. Her spirits revived, Rosemary said, "All the same, the poor vicar's daughter must despair of having you return with your heart intact. She will surely assume that your affections are now engaged by some pretty face you've met here in London."

"She will not," Broderick objected, casting her a sidelong glance. "I was engaged when I left the country—to you! She will hardly expect me to be mooning over 'some pretty face' as you call it, when I am supposed to be getting married at the end of the season."

"But were you to find your affections . . . engaged . . . would it be to some quiet, gently bred female or someone more vivacious?"

"Fishing, Rosie?"

Rosemary blushed deeply and studied her lap with more attention than it deserved.

"I'll be frank," Broderick went on. "I find most of the females I've met here to be rather tedious. I daresay that most of them find me to be a dead bore too."

"That's not true! Clarissa is continually singing your praises. She says you are handsome *and* the most interesting man of her acquaintance." She watched him closely to see if he flushed when she mentioned Clarissa's name.

"Flummery," he replied. Then on a more sober note, he added, "I am glad that she is your particular friend. I find her to be very amiable, and her brother is a good sort as well. I'd rather see you buckled to him than Beverley."

She ignored this comment, as she was too busy contemplating a list of attractive young ladies to whom Broderick had been introduced, and pondering which of them might be the owner of the purloined glove. If not Miss Thatcher or Clarissa, then whom?

"Let us get back to the subject of your earl and his catalogue of vices."

"You want me to marry someone prim and prosy?" Rosemary taunted.

"No, nor do I want you to marry in such a way that

you'll be ostracized by society," he told her with a frown. "I realize now that your plan will not work at all. In fact, it was doomed to failure at the start. I was too much of a cabbagehead to know that when you talked me into the scheme, but I know it now. What I can't figure is how you ever thought Beverley would make you an *honorable* offer when you were already engaged to me?"

Rosemary glanced frantically around for her grandmother as Broderick warmed to his subject.

"Confound it, Rosie! It just isn't done. Don't you see? The earl will never come up to scratch with me in the way. Unless of course, he elopes with you to Gretna Green. A man of his reputation would do such a thing, but is that what *you* want? A long carriage ride to Scotland in the middle of the night, to marry over an anvil?"

Rosemary opened her mouth and closed it again. The very thought of eloping to Scotland with Lord Beverley was repugnant. She shook her head vigorously, unable to speak.

"I find it more strange than I can say that he has not come forth to meet me face to face. If I had intended to make some female an offer, and she was swept right from under my nose, I can tell you, I'd be more than a littler curious to see the man that beat me out."

"Ricky, I don't think—"

"I've racked my brains trying to find a way to set you free of your obligation, so that Beverley can have another go. It's going to break Gordon's heart, I can tell you. And your mama—she may well go into a decline. But I dare say that once the earl comes up to scratch, she'll be right as rain again."

In that instant, Rosemary caught sight of Gordon escorting her grandmother into the gallery. She sighed heavily, rose and cast her grandmother an imploring glance. But it was Gordon who hastened to her side with eager intent.

"Roses!" He gave a disapproving snort as he surveyed the nearest watercolor canvas. He took Rosemary by the arm and led her away from Broderick.

"What's wrong with roses, Uncle Gordon?"

"Too tame, my dear. Too ordinary. That's what's wrong with them. Give me a tropical bird of paradise any day. Or a hibiscus or one of those orchids Broderick is so fond of."

Glancing over his shoulder and seeing that Emily and Broderick were engaged in a brisk discussion about the painting of poppies, he whispered, "I see that you are none the worse for our misadventure last night."

"Shhhh. We're not to speak of it. Remember?"

"Quite right. That place—those people. Mad as Bedlam! Rick was well out of it."

A moment or two later, Gordon and Broderick ran into an acquaintance—a gentleman and fellow member of the Royal Horticultural Society. Introductions were made all around and while the men spoke of an upcoming lecture, Rosemary took advantage of an opportunity to have a private word with her grandmother. "Gran, you must talk to Rick alone as soon as possible. He told me he has become so frustrated with my failed plan that he has considered having a word with Lord Beverley— on my behalf!" Rosemary's face was ashen.

"He must do no such thing!" Her grandmother pulled Rosemary into a more private corner.

"And so I told him. But still, we must take him into our confidence as soon as possible. I could not bear . . . it is *unthinkable* that Ricky should tell his lordship about my harebrained scheme. Particularly now—after what happened. I am sick with apprehension."

"I'll have a word with Broderick—alone."

"Oh, what a muddle!" Rosemary said, sighing.

"Better a muddle than a lawsuit," her grandmother threw in.

"What do you mean?"

"Breach of promise. As you are still a minor, I don't believe it will be a problem, but all the same we will want Broderick's assurance that there will be no suit brought against your poor mama."

Rosemary was stunned. "I hardly considered . . . I never thought—"

"No, you did not think. But trust me, when there is a fortune as considerable as yours, these matters can get out of hand."

"I know Rick would not consider such a scheme, and surely Uncle Gordon would not."

"But what about Sir Stephen? Perhaps he has expectations and is counting on the nuptials to occur so that he might bring them to fruition." Seeing Rosemary's dismal countenance, she hastened to add, "Do not worry your head about it, Rosemary. I will take care of everything. Leave it to me. You did not consider the consequences of your wild scheme—but we'll speak no more about that. We must focus our attention now on bringing the curtain down on your silly play."

"You do have a plan," Rosemary declared softly. She searched her grandmother's calm countenance. "You do!"

Emily nodded. A mischievous smile played about her lips, but she said nothing to enlighten her. Later, when Sir Stephen's town carriage pulled up at the Addison residence, Emily hung back, waiting for Gordon, Rosemary and Broderick to get out first. When Broderick offered his hand to help her step out of the carriage, she gave him a coy smile and gripped his hand firmly. Whispering in his ear, she said, "What if I told you that Rosemary no longer wants to marry Beverley? That she is happy with arrangements as they are and is willing to follow through with them?"

Broderick fixed his piercing gaze to bear upon her face. Emily saw the flash in his dark eyes and was pleased.

Chapter Fourteen

An hour and a half later, as Emily Addison was scribbling a transitional paragraph in the morning room, the butler announced Mr. Loren. She was not surprised. She'd been expecting him.

"Sit down, Broderick. Will you have some biscuits? A glass of wine?" she asked, rising from her desk. "A dish of tea, perhaps?"

"Nothing, ma'am, thank you," he said, taking a seat. His face seemed pale beneath his tan and his eyes glowed rather fiercely with something akin to hope. "Do I interrupt your writing?"

"It can't be helped." She took a seat on the small sofa across from him. "I won't pretend you're here to see Rosie. Besides, she's not here. She's gone shopping with Clarissa Paige."

Suddenly, Broderick was on his feet. "Were you hoaxing me? About what you said earlier when I was helping you down from the carriage."

"Certainly not. Now sit down. I don't want to get a crick in my neck looking up at you. There is much to discuss and we must talk plainly. But first, you must agree that what we say here must remain private between us."

"Yes, certainly," Broderick replied, resuming his seat and running his hand through his dark locks.

"Don't go blabbing to Gordon either."

"I can keep a confidence," he replied stiffly. "What kind of bacon-brained fellow do you think I am?"

"You're a ninnyhammer. You and Rosemary both." If Broderick was surprised or offended, he gave no indication of either. Emily continued. "Rosemary told me about the pretense between you and the motive behind it. I know *everything*."

The silence following this announcement was complete. Broderick blinked once or twice, sighed heavily and then slumped in his seat. "We're in pretty queer stirrups," he confessed.

"Indeed, but I'm not going to ring a peal over your head, Broderick. I know it was Rosemary who concocted this bumblebath, and you simply went along with it. But how either of you could think Beverley would propose marriage to a respectable young woman already engaged, I cannot imagine!"

"I told her the very same, ma'am. Several times, in fact, and again this very afternoon at the painting exhibit.

It's a devil of a tangle. But now Rosie has changed her mind, you say? Can it be true that she no longer cares for her cursed earl?"

Emily ignored the question and went on with her scold. "Gladys is quite run of her legs with wedding preparations and Gordon and Sir Stephen have expended a great deal of time and expense turning you out to advantage. But neither you or Rosemary seem to have a single regard for her or Gordon or anyone else. Your foolishness quite puts me to the blush."

Broderick lowered his head, shame-faced. "That's the worst of it. I've not liked lying to Gordon and I told Rosie so at the outset." Looking up, he asked, "But what did you mean when you said that Rosie no longer wants to marry the earl?"

Again, Emily ignored his inquiry. Frowning fiercely, she went on: "Rosemary says you've considered having a word with Lord Beverley in private. Under no circumstances are you to do so."

"I'm not such a gudgeon as all that," Broderick said with a sheepish smile.

Emily snorted. "While we were at the gallery this afternoon, she begged me with some urgency to drop a word of warning in your ear. She has had a change of heart and does not wish to marry Beverley at all. She never did, really. It was a matter of pride—not a matter of the heart. When he did not ask for her hand at the end of last Season, Rosie was quite put out. Her indignation turned to anger and in an outraged muddle she hatched this odious scheme. You have been badly misused, Broderick, and I'm sorry for it."

"She told you outright that she no longer wishes to marry Beverley?"

"Yes, she was quite emphatic, and I believe her. This morning, she sent the bouquet Beverley sent as a token of his esteem down to the kitchen for the cook. Did she say anything at all to you about the matter?"

"No. She encouraged me to give a lecture and wanted to know if my head had been turned by any pretty face here in London. She even asked if I preferred quiet females or more vivacious ones."

"Minx," Emily said, chuckling. "She's in love with you, Broderick. She's too chagrined to admit it, but she is. What are you going to do about it?"

"If I thought . . . if only I could be certain . . ." Broderick jumped to his feet and paced the room like a caged animal. "Rosie never said a word this afternoon . . . about not pursuing his attentions."

"I told her not to say anything at all upon the matter. When Rosemary confessed her odious scheme, she asked me to help her out of this scrape. I agreed, but ordered her to say and do nothing until I'd given it some thought. The chit's woolly thinking—not to mention excessive pride—got her in this pickle in the first place."

"Knowing Rosie, she has some plan in mind."

"I believe she wants to break off the engagement so that you might return to Hodge Hall and your tropical plants."

"I've guessed that much—that she'd call off our engagement. But then what will she do?"

"Something very dramatic, I should think. She'll make herself ill and confine herself to bed, perhaps. Then she'll dwindle into a decline. She may even contract the smallpox or maybe scarlet fever. She'll ask me to accompany her to Bath. There will be camphor-soaked handkerchiefs and blinds drawn to keep out the sun. She'll play the part of an invalid with a broken heart and she'll do it quite well."

"Horrid little bouncer," Broderick declared, but he said it with such tenderness that Emily could not help grinning at him. Broderick grinned back at her. "You have quite an imagination, Mrs. Addison. I daresay your career as a romance novelist will be a successful one."

"Save your pretty speeches for Rosemary. I told her that the easiest course to pursue would be to go ahead with her marriage to you. What do you say to that? You do want to marry Rosemary, don't you? I am not in my dotage, you know. I have noticed the tender regard you have for her. I told her you would make her a good husband."

"What did she say to that?" Broderick asked hoarsely, fixing his attention upon a vase of flowers on the mantle.

"She said nothing. But she blushed and stammered and nearly burst into tears. She appeared so discomforted that I knew at once that she was in love with you. However, she's too proud to admit it, and she feels it would be the honorable thing to free you of your obligation and let you return to the country."

After a moment's consideration, Broderick said, "Perhaps Mrs. Addison would prefer another of Rosemary's suitors for a son-in-law. I am well aware that ours would not be an equal marriage. Rosie is an heiress and I have no consequence whatsoever."

"Humbug."

"One or two titled gentlemen offered marriage before Rosemary concocted her little plot, didn't they?"

Emily shrugged. "Nearer half a dozen, I should say," she exaggerated, "but Rosie dismissed them all without a second thought. Naturally, Gladys would like to boast that her daughter is a countess or better, but she was not displeased with the attachment between you. Surprised, of course, but not displeased. Do you doubt it?"

"A little."

"Put it out of your mind. My daughter-in-law may have cherished the idea of a title for Rosie at one time, but she'll be satisfied with Rosemary's choice of husband. And that, Broderick, is in your hands now. I'm relying on you not to make a muddle of it."

"I'm glad Rosemary's not planning to marry Beverley. He has a certain reputation, don't you know?"

"I do know," Emily said, a smile playing about her lips. Broderick took a seat next to her on the sofa. His brow puckered into a frown.

"Rosemary is young and her emotions . . . er . . ."—

he searched for the right word—"volatile. I wouldn't want to take advantage of her unsteady emotions. What if we do go through with this marriage and after a few months or even years Rosemary laments that she did not see the masquerade through to the finish?"

Emily leaned toward him. Patting his large brown hands with one of her smaller, frail ones, she smiled gently and said, "I have told you the truth, Broderick. Rosemary is in love with you. I know my granddaughter. The happiest she has even been in her life were those short weeks she spent in the country with you."

"It was the same for me, ma'am. Had I not been so besotted I would have recognized Rosie's foolish scheme for what it was. But she can be so . . . so persuasive. It's dashed difficult to say no."

"She turned sour-faced and ill-tempered almost as soon as we returned to London," Emily went on.

"She always appeared in full bloom," Broderick replied.

"In public, perhaps, not in private. She took no interest in wedding clothes and preparations. Why, she even struck the maid across the knuckles with a hairbrush!"

Broderick blinked once or twice before coming to Rosemary's defense. "She's suffering deep disappointment. It's been weeks and we've still not see Beverley."

Emily wisely said nothing about Rosemary's unfortunate encounter with the earl on the previous evening. "She's been miserable, not wanting to follow through with the masquerade and yet not knowing how to get out of the tangle." She rose and Broderick did the same.

"Woo the girl! And don't be hen-hearted about it. At present, we've got the cart before the horse, and it's a bit awkward, I'll admit. But you can bring it 'round, Broderick, and you may rely on me to give all the support I can."

When Broderick took his leave some fifteen minutes later, Emily heaved a sigh and returned to her writing desk. She'd promised Rosemary a happy ending and now felt assured that one would soon be forthcoming. She only hoped she could do the same for the forlorn heroine in her novel-in-progress. She was still struggling with conflict resolution an hour later when she heard Rosemary's voice in the hall and that of her daughter-in-law as well. Leaving the morning room, Emily nearly collided with a passing footman teetering under a pile of hatboxes and packages.

"Rosemary, you look feverish," Emily declared, noting the bright red spots on her granddaughter's cheeks.

"You do look flushed. Are you feeling quite all right?" Gladys asked, peering at her.

Rosemary smiled weakly and removed her hat. "I'm just tired, Mama." Turning to Emily, she asked, "Do we interrupt your composition?"

"I have been plotting," Emily said, a smile playing about her lips.

"Plotting what?" Gladys asked, removing her gloves.

"A happy ending," she replied. Rosemary regarded

her with widened eyes and her flush deepened. "For my novel," Emily added.

"Rosemary, your grandmother is quite right. You do look feverish," Gladys declared, staring at her with some concern. "Do you have a sore throat? Does your head ache?"

"It's nothing, Mama, really. I'm just tired and it is overly warm today as well."

"We have Sir Stephen's supper party this evening," her mother reminded her. "Perhaps you should take a nap."

"I'll do that, Mama. I want a word with Gran, and then I'll go straight up."

Gladys nodded briskly and passed down the hall. Rosemary hurried her grandmother into the morning room and whispered, "Tell me, Gran, what have you been plotting?"

With a cautious eye to the door, Emily explained briefly that Broderick had stopped by. "I've had a word with him. We can count on Broderick not to do anything foolish where Lord Beverley is concerned."

Rosemary heaved a sigh of relief. Embracing her grandmother with fervor, she said, "Thank you, Gran. That's one worry off my mind. What did he say? Was he surprised? Is he angry? Does he think I'm a fickle peahen? What are we going to do now?"

"We'll discuss it later. You do look feverish, and I'm certain you could use a nap. You're not sick, are you?"

"No, just tired, and embarrassed," Rosemary told her.

When Emily arched her brows inquiringly, she explained. "Clarissa asked, with utmost delicacy, if I was having bridesmaids in the wedding, and that's when I realized that I'd not asked her to be my maid of honor. I told her—can you believe it?—that it had slipped my mind, that of course I wanted her to be my maid of honor." Rosemary sighed. "Of course, we had to see the dressmaker. We can now add Clarissa to the list of those who will be heartbroken when we put an end to this shameful masquerade."

Emily clasped her gently by the shoulders and said softly, "If you were willing to wed Broderick in earnest, this would all come out right as rain."

Blushing, Rosemary stared down at the buckle on her shoe. "Gran, I told you that was not possible."

"Yes, I believe you did, but you failed to say *why.*"

There was a considerable silence before Rosemary responded in a near whisper, "Ricky has formed a passion for another."

Stunned, Emily said nothing at first. "How do you know this?" she finally asked.

With quivering lips and tears sparkling in her blue eyes, Rosemary said, "He carries her glove—a love token—in his breast pocket over his heart."

Chapter Fifteen

Despite the attractions at Vauxhall Gardens, Rosemary found she could think of little else but her unfortunate dilemma. Her grandmother had been momentarily stunned by the unexpected revelation about the glove, but had made Rosemary promise not to do anything to further complicate matters. Rosemary had given her promise, but she couldn't help fretting and feeling melancholy whenever she considered the certainty that Broderick and Uncle Gordon would very soon be returning to the country—just as soon as the mock engagement had been called off.

Rosemary smoothed the skirt of her new sapphire-blue frock and knew she looked quite stunning. Everyone said so. It was part of her wedding trousseau, but she took little pleasure in it. Broderick was complete to a shade in a frilled shirt, satin knee breeches and silk stockings. She'd never seen him look so handsome. When he took her hand and raised it to his lips, she said lightly, "Ricky, I fear you're becoming a practiced flirt."

"And I fear I'm in need of *more* practice. Since coming to London, we have scarcely enjoyed a moment alone. I hope to remedy that." He then smiled at her so warmly, Rosemary blushed with confusion and looked away—but not before glancing surreptitiously at his breast pocket.

She wondered if he carried the treasured glove with him this evening and to whom it might belong. She'd considered every marriageable female of her acquaintance. As none seemed the likely owner of the purloined glove, she was ready to conclude that it was the property of a pretty bit o' muslin that Broderick had met on the streets of London. With a disapproving sniff, Rosemary dismissed this thought and resolved to enjoy the evening and not dwell on Broderick's love token or its mysterious owner.

The party proved to be a merry one with her grandmother and mother in attendance, as well as Mr. Nevin, Uncle Gordon and Captain Percival Lewis and his unmarried sister, Miss Patience Lewis, particular friends of Sir Stephen, their host. That gentleman had ordered an extravagant quantity of chicken and ham—for which the gardens were famous—and an assortment of sweets and comfits. There was lemonade for the ladies and port for the gentlemen.

"Gran, I have an idea," Rosemary whispered, taking her grandmother aside while the rest of the party filled their plates. "I've been contemplating my dilemma and may know a way to resolve it."

Arching a skeptical eyebrow, Emily regarded her granddaughter thoughtfully.

Rosemary continued. "I shall become quite ill. You will take me to Oakley—no, Bath. We shall then let out the story that I have released Broderick from our engagement, as there is so little hope for my recovery."

Emily sputtered and nearly dropped her lemonade goblet. "Rosemary, put the notion out of your head at once!" she said sharply. "I cannot imagine you confined to your room for months on end, playing the invalid. Only consider, there would be no parties, no dancing, no riding, no shopping! Besides, I cannot think such a melancholy scheme would convince your mother to marry Mr. Nevin and leave with him for India."

"That's true. Mama would not leave me," Rosemary said with a heavy sigh.

"Rosemary, you promised—no more scheming."

"But, Gran, it's so hard to sit idle and do nothing."

"That's just what I expect you to do, Rosemary—nothing!" Emily frowned at her sternly. Rosemary shrugged. She would have protested more vigorously, but at that moment Miss Lewis appeared beside them. The young woman had a pleasant countenance and a fine pair of gray eyes.

"Miss Addison, your mother tells me that you and Mr.

Loren will voyage to Botany Bay for your wedding trip. It's a place I've always wished to see. When do you sail?"

Embarrassed, Rosemary stammered, "I'm . . . er . . . not quite sure really. I've left all the details to Rick— Broderick."

Emily hastened to her granddaughter's rescue. "Do you enjoy traveling, Miss Lewis?"

"Indeed," she replied and proceeded to amaze both Emily and Rosemary with details of her recent journey to Egypt. "I often accompany my brother when he has military duties to perform. We visited Italy last winter too."

"Did you see the pyramids in Egypt?" Rosemary asked, regarding her new acquaintance with frank interest.

"Yes, from the back of a camel," Miss Lewis replied with a smile. "A creature I could never grow fond of, I'm afraid."

"And what took you to Italy, Miss Lewis? Business or pleasure?" Gladys Addison asked, stepping into their circle to join the conversation. She smiled at Rosemary before adding, somewhat shyly, "With my own upcoming journey to India, I find I'm quite eager to discuss travel these days."

Rosemary felt a rush of guilt and dismay as she considered her mother's eager expression.

"My brother has a retired military friend living near Naples," Miss Lewis explained. "He's wanted Percy to visit for quite some time. When Dr. Jenner asked us to deliver some of his vaccine to a medical acquaintance there, we decided to kill two birds with one stone, as they say. Speaking of birds, we carried the lymph in the quill of a bird's feather, don't you know?"

"Dr. Edward Jenner?" Emily asked, intrigued. "I've read his pamphlet on the prevention of smallpox by using cowpox lymph. It's rather controversial."

"Is it true that a woman who received the vaccine later gave birth to a bovanized infant?" Gladys pursued, with several nervous blinks.

"What does bovanized mean?" Rosemary asked.

"The child was born with a cow tail or was it a cow head?" her mother asked, looking at them all in turn.

"That's merely a vicious rumor," Miss Lewis declared. "It is being spread by members of the anti-vaccination leagues. These people are dangerous. They have convinced large portions of the population not to have their children vaccinated, urging them to keep their blood pure. It's a crime, I say."

Rosemary listened raptly as Patience Lewis defended Dr. Jenner's procedure. She was keenly aware that although Miss Lewis was only a few years older than she was, Miss Lewis had seen and done so much more. She was, Rosemary feared, the kind of woman Broderick would find interesting and attractive. Next to her, she felt embarrassingly ignorant. Not for the first time, Rosemary realized that there was more to life than being rich and beautiful. When Miss Lewis mentioned that it was Dr. Jenner who had first piqued her brother Percival's interest in hydrogen balloons, Rosemary felt compelled to speak.

"I have seen such a balloon, Miss Lewis! It was immense! Uncle Gordon, Broderick and I chased them across the countryside on horseback. It was great fun! The two gentlemen inside the basket landed in a field not far from our home in the country."

"You never told me, my dear? When was this?" Gladys asked, turning to her daughter.

"When she was at Oakley, on her repairing lease," Emily said dryly.

Rosemary blushed, but was spared the discomfort of explaining. Miss Lewis, enthusiastic about the subject, mentioned that her brother owned such a balloon. "Only recently we filled it with hydrogen in the courtyard at Berkeley Castle," she explained. "It's not large enough to be manned, but it was great fun, as you say, Miss Addison, following after it across the countryside. It traveled ten miles before landing in a field and frightening the startled reapers."

The women laughed. Gladys then excused herself to seek out more refreshment, while Emily claimed Broderick's arm for a walk to view the nearest fountain. As the lanterns in the garden were lit and the orchestra began to play in the pavilion, the park took on a more festive atmosphere. "I've never done anything exciting," Rosemary lamented. "I've never even been to Scotland."

"You are quite young, Miss Addison," her new friend told her with a sweet smile.

"I'm not sure I'm prepared for adventure," Rosemary went on. "I can do needlework and play the pianoforte a little."

At that moment, she heard Broderick's robust laugh. She quickly turned her head and noticed her grandmother laughing with him. They were too far away for her to hear their humorous discussion, but she had a sinking suspicion that the joke had been made at her expense.

Miss Lewis, noticing Rosemary's distraction, said, "What's the jest, I wonder?"

Rosemary felt ridiculously put out. She also felt naïve, foolish and ignorant. It made her waspish. Putting down her plate, she asked crisply, "Miss Lewis, forgive me for being forward, but have you never thought of marrying?" She regretted the words as soon as she'd spoken them.

Patience Lewis was taken aback. "Why certainly, Miss Addison. What woman does not? I have been asked—twice—but as my grandmother left me with a modest inheritance, there is no need for me to make a marriage of convenience, and I did not like either gentleman well enough to marry."

"You mean you did not love them?" Rosemary corrected her.

Miss Lewis nodded. "I did not love them nor did I like them either. I think friendship is the most important element in a marriage. Love blossoms later, after the friendship has put down deeper roots."

Rosemary pondered this and realized there was some truth in it. She'd once considered that she'd loved Lord Beverley, but she'd been misled by frivolous emotions. The friendship she had for Broderick had deep roots that had—suddenly and inconveniently—blossomed into love.

"I understand you and Mr. Loren were childhood playmates," Miss Lewis went on. "He seems to me a sensible and amiable man."

"He is," Rosemary replied. Her voice sounded hoarse.

"That is what I meant about marrying one's friend. You *like* Mr. Loren. Over the years, you've come to like him more and more."

Rosemary blushed to the roots of her hair. "Yes, I like him very much," she confessed. Recalling their time together in the country—the strawberry picking and their daily rides, their time together in the greenhouse—she realized that those weeks had been the happiest of her life. "He's so very agreeable that he read Miss Austen's *Sense and Sensibility* just to please me," she added proudly.

"Well, there you are! You know what I mean exactly. One day, should I meet a gentleman as agreeable as Mr. Loren, and if that gentleman should have the good sense to ask for my hand in marriage, than I will wed, Miss Addison." She paused and, looking down at her hands, shrugged and said, "But enough of this. I don't want to bore you into lethargy."

"Indeed, you will not, Miss Lewis. May I call you

Patience? And would you be good enough to call me Rosemary? I feel as though we are to be great friends."

The two continued their animated conversation and were soon joined by Emily and Broderick, their faces flushed with laughter. Broderick was eager to hear of the Lewis' balloon and Sir Stephen urged his guests again to partake of the sumptuous repast. When Lord Beverley, most elegantly attired and carrying a new silver snuffbox, strolled casually by with his friend Mr. Alfred Falkner, Rosemary nearly choked on a sliver of ham. She kept her attention fixed upon her plate. Still, she could feel his blue-eyed gaze sweep across her like the touch of a fingertip. She was annoyed, rather than pleased by it.

"Good evening, Merrimam," the earl said.

Sir Stephen acknowledged him with a friendly nod and proceeded—much to Rosemary's agitation—to acquaint Beverley and Falkner with the members of the party to whom they'd not been previously introduced. Mr. Nevin rose to his feet, as did Gordon and Broderick, who looked the earl over critically before holding out his hand. Rosemary held her breath.

"I've heard a great deal about you," Broderick said.

For an agonizing instant, Rosemary thought she would sink. Her grandmother chose that opportune moment to prod her in the back with her folded fan. Rosemary flinched, remembering her grandmother's earlier admonition to behave "like an Addison."

"Have you indeed?" the earl drawled, eyeing Broderick through his quizzing glass.

"You've been lucky at cards, we hear," Gordon said.

"Everyone's talking of your immense good fortune at the gaming tables, Beverley," Sir Stephen added.

"Quite a run of luck," Broderick put in.

The earl nodded. "Indeed."

There followed what Rosemary considered an awkward moment of silence, as though the two men were taking each other's measure. Comparing the two, she admitted to herself that the earl was undoubtedly a nonpareil, but Broderick was taller and far more personable. She could not deny that the earl was handsome, like the hero in a fairy tale that schoolgirls read about. But Broderick was handsome too in a rugged, manly sort of way. Besides, he was kind, good-natured and considerate. He would never kiss a girl on the mouth when he was foxed!

"Tom's not the only one everyone's talking about," Falkner said, trying to sound jolly. "Mr. Bugs and Mr. Buds coming from America and the latter securing the hand of the most beautiful heiress in London," he said with a gallant bow in Rosemary's direction. Then turning to Broderick, he added, "I wish you happy, Mr. Loren."

"May I offer my own felicitations on your good fortune," Beverley said, bowing stiffly.

As Broderick graciously murmured a polite thank

you, Gordon asked the earl if he preferred whist or pi-
quet. When Sir Stephen interrupted, pulling Broderick
and Gordon aside to introduce them to another acquaintance, the earl made use of the opportunity to approach
Rosemary. Leaning close, he said in her ear, "I trust
you received the small token of my esteem earlier today."

Rosemary, who was seated, looked up into his face.
His lips curled with a knowing smile. His eyes glittered.
She found his smug manner annoying, and her immediate discomfort at his unnerving proximity turned to indignation.

"Do you mean that hodgepodge bouquet of wild flowers, my lord?" she asked quietly, not wanting her mother
or Miss Lewis, sitting behind her, to overhear. In the
frozen silence that ensued, she was pleased to see his
eyes narrow ever so slightly. A frown replaced his lazy
smile. When the earl cast a cautionary glance at Emily
Addison, who sat next to her at the table, Rosemary followed his gaze and declared, "I have no secrets from
my grandmother."

Emily, leaning forward, confirmed this statement with
a chilly smile.

"As for your token of esteem, I sent it to the kitchen,
for the cook's pleasure," Rosemary remarked heart-
lessly. "I am sure it is more to her liking than mine."
Rising, she excused herself and cast a brief, imploring
glance at her grandmother. On quaking legs, Rosemary
made her way to Broderick's side. She slipped her arm

through his in a possessive manner and greeted Sir Stephen's newly arrived friends with such a dazzling smile that those gentlemen found themselves thinking young Loren very fortunate indeed.

Beverley watched for a moment before turning his attention to Rosemary's grandmother. Emily slowly fluttered her fan. "Rosemary prefers orchids, my lord, particularly Mr. Loren's. Surely you knew?" Her eyes fixed him with a silent, unmistakable challenge.

"I beg your pardon," Beverley said, bowing stiffly.

"Give me your arm, my lord," Emily said, rising. "Shall we walk a bit?" With her fan, she indicated a lighted path lined with rose bushes. "I could fall back on an old woman's privilege of being uncivil, but I will not. You have made a mistake, but I'm certain you will not make the same mistake again."

"And what mistake might that be, Mrs. Addison?" he inquired with a lazy drawl.

"Last night's misadventure was nothing more than a girlish escapade," Emily said with a shrug.

"You know about last night?" Beverley asked. His frown deepened.

"Certainly. Did not my granddaughter just say that she has no secrets from me? After scolding her heartily for her indiscretion and rebuking Mr. Stanley-Hodge for being henwitted, we enjoyed a laugh about it. Particularly Mr. Loren," she lied, giving him a sly, sidelong glance.

"What else did she tell you, ma'am?"

"That you kissed her, and I'm quite vexed about it. Furthermore, Rosemary said you were foxed," Emily replied.

"She could tell it?" the Earl inquired with an odd laugh.

"She could *smell* it, my lord. Of course, we did not tell Mr. Loren of your vulgar behavior. He would dislike it excessively. If I did not think you were contrite and regretted your unseemly conduct, my lord, I would box your ears."

There was a short frozen silence before Beverley said, "I believe you would."

But Emily was not yet done with him. She turned and caused him to do the same. "Look at them. See how well they suit one another."

Beverley followed her gaze. Rosemary and Broderick did look well together—a handsome couple and so at ease in one another's company. Rosemary's hand rested lightly on Broderick's arm. He'd covered her hand with one of his own and appeared to caress it absently.

"A love match, as you can see," Emily pointed out.

After studying the young couple briefly, Beverley murmured, "Perhaps I *am* a gudgeon after all."

"And a slow top, sir—or is it simply *slow*?" Emily replied with a crack of mirth.

Beverley chuckled humorlessly. Strolling slowly toward the supper box, he asked, "How would it be if you told me the truth, ma'am? I'm not such a gudgeon that

I believe Rosemary . . . er . . . Miss Addison retired to the country on a repairing lease. She was in the bloom of health when she left London, I'd swear to it."

"Mr. Loren and Mr. Stanley-Hodge had recently returned from America, as you know. Rosemary and Broderick have been childhood friends, and she was impatient to see him."

"The engagement was all so sudden—so unexpected. Something doesn't fudge. Mrs. Addison, your daughter-in-law, never hinted at such an attachment."

"Why should Gladys have hinted at anything to you, I wonder?" Emily stopped walking and turned to face him. Her eyes were kindling. "You, after all, are only one of Rosemary's many admirers and certainly not the most sincere. You are a rake, my lord! Your behavior last night is a shocking example of the decay of modern morals."

Although Beverley said nothing, his frown deepened and a muscle quivered at the corner of his mouth. Emily straightened her shoulders and made a final thrust. "How grateful I am that my granddaughter's *generous fortune* has allowed her to marry where she will!"

She pierced him with an icy stare. Ignoring her scowl, he refreshed himself with a pinch of snuff and then offered her his arm. "Ma'am, I shall return you to your party."

"Obliged, I'm sure," she quipped.

Lord Beverley returned her to the supper box and the smiling company of her daughter-in-law and Miss

Lewis. Emily gave him one last penetrating stare. He bowed to her with his usual grace. He smiled lazily at Gladys Addison and Patience Lewis and bowed to them as well, wishing them a good evening.

"Enjoy the fireworks," he drawled, exchanging a final glance at Emily. "I certainly have."

Chapter Sixteen

Rosemary noticed the Earl's departure and left Broderick chatting with Sir Stephen's acquaintances to hurry to her grandmother's side. "Gran, what did you say to him? What did *he* say? What do we do now?" she asked in a whispered rush.

Emily nibbled a small strawberry tart and glanced around cautiously. Assured that she could not be overheard, she replied, "I gave him a civil set down, and he bowed out graciously."

"How brave you are!"

"You'll have nothing to fear from that direction, I can assure you," Emily went on with a nod.

Rosemary heaved a sigh and nearly crumbled into the chair next to her grandmother's. "I am relieved to hear it. I have worried myself sick, fancying all sorts of troubles."

"Ninnyhammer," Emily chided as she took a sip of lemonade.

Rosemary rushed on. "I've never been more relieved in my life. I shudder to think I might have made such a misalliance. I cannot conceive what a fool I was to fancy myself in love with him. I hope I shall never set eyes upon him again!"

"Of course, you shall. When you do, be merely polite and move on. What a widgeon you are, Rosemary!"

"Don't scold, Gran." Reaching for her own goblet, she took a sip of lemonade and started to ask what manner of joke her grandmother and Broderick had shared earlier in the evening. She was reluctant to do so, fearing that the jest had been at her expense. She did not want that fear confirmed. It hurt to think that Rick would laugh at her. Instead, she confided, "I was worried that Broderick would say or do something foolish when he was introduced to Lord Beverley."

"Broderick? Do something foolish?" Emily asked with severity. "What did you think he might do? Challenge Beverley to a duel? If Broderick is guilty of doing anything foolhardy, it was only to please you. Generally, he's a very sensible young man. Suggest anything otherwise, and I shall be all out of sorts with you."

Rosemary fell silent. She felt more than a little hurt that her grandmother, of late, seemed to take Broderick's side in all things. She had reached for a comfit but withdrew her hand. She'd suddenly lost her appetite.

"My girl, you are young, and I suppose that is why

you cannot comprehend the scandal that your ill-fated escapade could have embroiled the family in." Emily stood and looked down upon her granddaughter. "Why, I have half a mind to—" She turned away, leaving the supper box to join Patience Lewis, Gladys and Gordon, who stood upon the grass watching acrobats perform near the gazebo.

Rosemary lowered her head and blinked back hot tears that threatened to spill down her cheeks. She was overcome by regret—forcing Broderick to leave his beloved greenhouse to join her in London, lying to her mother and Clarissa Paige, and deceiving Uncle Gordon. She even regretted that Broderick was unable to name his new orchid after her glove. A silly inconsequential thing that, but it saddened her still. Hearing Broderick's laugh, she turned her head. Her heart ached at the sound of it. She studied his broad back and long, well-muscled legs. How handsome he was! Soon, he would return to Hodge Hall. She would miss not only his laughter, but his companionship as well.

As though able to read her thoughts, Broderick turned suddenly and fixed his fine dark eyes upon her. Rosemary swallowed hard and forced a smile. He came toward her, moving with such manly grace that Rosemary could not help but stare with admiration. Sitting down next to her, he leaned forward and whispered, "Egads, Rosie, what a night! I finally met your elusive earl. Quite a buck of the first head!" he declared with a grin.

"Ssshhh!" she warned, glancing around cautiously.

"He's a hateful wretch! He sent the most horrid bouquet of flowers."

"Then it is no wonder you despise him!" Broderick laughed, accepting a glass of port from the waiter hovering nearby.

"You have no idea what a quake I was in when he presented himself. I was afraid of what you might say or do."

"You think I'm still such a bumpkin that I'd make a cake of myself in public?" he asked with a frown.

She blushed with shame. "No, I didn't mean that, exactly."

"What did you mean?" Then noting her sagging shoulders and air of gentle melancholy, he asked, "What's the matter, Rosie? Are you tired?"

"Yes, I'm quite dead with fatigue," she replied and meant it. The anxiety of the past several weeks had begun to take its toll.

"Shall I take you home?"

Rosemary started to answer and then realized that the evening's festivities had been planned for his benefit. "But Ricky, you haven't seen the Chinese pavilion or the fountains and the fireworks," she protested feebly.

"No matter. I've had enough frivolity for one evening."

"And so have I," Gordon exclaimed, joining them at the table. "I'm near dead on my feet. Too old for all this gadding about!" He gave Rosemary a wink. She smiled back at him. She knew he was alluding to their secret excursion to the masquerade. She knew also that the tall old gentlemen would find vigor cnough if the evening activities included bug collecting.

"My dear Mr. Bugs," she said, grinning up at him. "And Mr. Buds," she added, turning to Broderick. "I know how the both of you must long for the quiet, studious evenings at Hodge Hall."

"You've never said a truer word, my dear!" Gordon declared. Broderick said nothing, which only pricked Rosemary's conscience more than had he openly agreed. As Gordon prattled on about all the insect mounting that awaited his attention back at the Hall, Rosemary listened inattentively and Broderick went to speak to Sir Stephen about their early departure. She tucked her lower lip under her front teeth and worried about how her grandmother could possibly bring all to a satisfying conclusion.

In the barouche on the way home, Broderick held her hand and smiled at her as though he knew a secret. "Shall we go riding in the park tomorrow? Just the two of us?"

"I'd like that," she said, knowing it may well be one of the last outings they would enjoy together.

However, on the following morning, Rosemary awoke to heavy rain streaming down her bedroom windows. She was cast immediately into the doldrums. She took a light breakfast of toast and tea in her room before donning a new morning dress of pink muslin with an embroidered flounce and tight sleeves buttoned at the wrist. But even the new frock didn't cheer her up. With her mother gone out with Mr. Nevin and her grandmother absent as well, the house on fashionable Albemarle Street seemed lonely and over large. Restless, she roamed from one room to the next. When she entered the billiards room that had once been her father's favorite room in the house, she decided to play a solitary game.

She hadn't thought about her deceased parent for some years, and doing so now only increased her burden of guilt. Not only was she a selfish and deceiving friend, she was a thoughtless daughter as well! Conscience-stricken, Rosemary felt heartily ashamed of herself. She blinked back anguished tears and succumbed to her low sprits, acknowledging that her tally of sins was considerable. She'd lied to Clarissa, her best friend in the entire world. She'd deceived her own mother and grandmother and dear Uncle Gordon. She'd done even worse to Broderick, for she'd made him a co-conspirator in her devious but cork-brained scheme.

Using the back of her hand to swipe at the tears on her cheeks, she glanced at the rain streaming down the windows and sighed. She would not be able to go riding with Broderick after all—not in this downpour—and the thought made her even more depressed. After all, she had very little time left to spend with him and she wanted to cherish every opportunity between now and the time he returned to Hodge Hall.

When the butler announced Mr. Broderick Loren a scant twenty minutes later, Rosemary received him with surprised delight. He strode in through the door with a broad smile on his handsome face. Raindrops glistened in his dark hair and upon his bottle-green coat.

"Good morning, Rosie! How pretty you look! Bracing weather," he observed cheerfully.

"Miserable weather, you mean," she said with a pout. She tugged him by the sleeve toward the fire. "You'll catch your death," she scolded as she helped him to remove his coat.

"Your cheeks are blooming likes roses, but your hands are cold," Broderick said, capturing hers and rubbing them between his own. Rosemary, noting that his eyes appeared unnaturally bright, fixed her unsteady gaze upon his crumbled cravat. "I hope the weather clears by tomorrow," he went on. "I've been invited to view the construction of Percival Lewis' new balloon."

At this announcement, Rosemary's face brightened. "Oh, Ricky, may I come too? Will Patience be there? Is it the basket or the envelope that is under construction?" Noting his surprise, she tilted her head to one side and quipped, "I've learned a lot about ballooning since last evening. I believe I would like to have one of my own. And I'd like to go up in it too—but only if it is safely tethered on the ground."

"Rosie, you're full of pluck!" Broderick declared, his eyes gleaming with admiration.

The warmth in his gaze disconcerted her. She returned to the billiards table. Reaching for her stick, she blurted out, "My charade has gone sadly awry, but I'm not sorry for it. It was to be expected. It was a silly plan in the first place."

"Indeed, it was."

"As I told Gran last evening, I shudder to think what a fool I was to fancy myself in love with him—Lord Beverley," she went on, leaning over the table and taking a shot.

"You're quite certain—that you're not in love with him?" Broderick asked, reaching for a stick of his own.

"Of that you can be sure," Rosemary declared warmly.

"I'm glad to hear it, Rosie. After meeting him last night, I'll grant you, he's a handsome rascal. But he has a poor reputation. I realize now why you thought you could convince the devil to elope with you to Gretna Green. However, I would be interested to know what wiles you would have employed to cajole him into taking you over the border." He arched an eyebrow.

Rosemary blushed and lowered her gaze. "I hadn't thought that far ahead at the time I made my henwitted scheme," she admitted.

"That I can easily believe!" Broderick declared. "I can't think why mothers with marriageable daughters have laid siege to the man for the past ten years. He has no fortune—only a title."

"I do not care what he has—or has not," Rosemary said, moving around the table and regarding the balls. "He means nothing to me at all."

"Then I hope I'll be able to make myself agreeable to you, although we are uncomfortably situated in our present predicament."

Rosemary looked at him, confused. "Ricky, I do find you agreeable. I like you more than anyone else of my acquaintance," she admitted with naive frankness. "Even more than Gran and Clarissa."

"Thank heaven for that," he murmured, watching a ball roll slowly into a side pocket.

"I've tried my best to think of some way to bring down the curtain on this play, but I cannot. We'll have to rely on Gran. All I can think of is retiring for a season to Bath and falling ill with something serious, like scarlet fever."

"Or smallpox perhaps," Broderick suggested, a good deal amused.

Rosemary looked up and nodded eagerly. "Yes, just so."

Broderick chuckled. "Your grandmother, who pities me for having been so badly misused by you, warned me that you might come up with another bacon-brained plot."

"She did not!" Rosemary put down her cue stick with some force.

"She did! She went so far as drawing a vivid picture, with 'camphor-soaked hankies' and 'blinds drawn against the sun' or something like."

For a moment, Rosemary was speechless. Then she giggled and, lowering her head, covered her flushed face with one hand.

"I don't find it amusing," Broderick went on. "What kind of shabby fellow do you think I am that I'd not love you enough to see you through an illness—till death do us part, remember?" he said warmly. "Besides, Gordon would tear me limb from limb for abandoning you in such a manner."

"Broderick, I know you feel honor-bound not to draw back from our . . . our arrangement," Rosemary said, giving up the game and moving to the fire. "But we must think of a way. Perhaps you could dally after some lightskirt, and I could pretend to be offended beyond any hope of reconciliation."

"Rosie! To think I'd ever hear such a word on your lips."

"But it might serve," she insisted. "It shouldn't damage your reputation either, Ricky. In fact, it might well enhance it. I could act like a shrew for several months and no one would blame you for seeking . . . er . . . consolation elsewhere."

"I wonder I don't wring your neck," Broderick mumbled, watching as she took a shot. Moving around the table toward her, he said, "Rosemary, you're laboring under the misapprehension that I want to be let out of our engagement."

There was a moment or two of frozen silence before Rosemary declared with conviction, "Good gracious, Ricky, you've gone mad! Your generous offer does you honor, but you need not marry me. I never meant for you to . . . to . . ." Her much-moved voice quavered.

"No, Rosie, I'm not mad. I *was* so when I allowed myself to be talked into your hare-brained scheme, but not now. Not at this moment. Over the past several weeks, I've come to realize that I do not want to cut the knot between us." When she said nothing, he took another step closer. "You are worthy of a better man than I am, darling, but I love you." He lifted her hand to his lips and kissed it.

A knot in her throat made it difficult to speak. "It's impossible," she choked and pulled her hand from his warm grasp.

"No, it is not. Your grandmother led me to believe that you were not indifferent to me, that you would favor my suit. Obviously, she was mistaken," he said stiffly.

Rosemary didn't look at him, but she could feel his eyes searching her face. When he said, "I have something to return to you," she did glance up. Broderick placed his stick on the table and went to retrieve something from the pocket of his coat that was drying on the back of a chair near the fire. He pressed it to his lips and handed it over to its rightful owner. "This belongs to you," he said.

Rosemary stared at him incredulously before slowly taking the glove from him. She was prepared to contradict him but gave a nervous laugh as she examined it and realized that it was indeed one of her own. She flushed to the roots of her hair. Her head reeled. So did her heart.

"How did you come by this?" she asked huskily.

Broderick took a step closer. "I can tell you the exact day, the specific hour and the precise moment. If you must know."

"But . . . why?" she asked with a tremble in her voice.

"Because I like to pretend that your hand is in that glove, resting over my heart," he said softly.

They confronted one another with a good deal of awkwardness. His long fingers closed over her hand, the one that clutched the purloined glove. A smile trembled on Rosemary's lips. Her eyes full of tender laughter, she said, "Oh, Rick, Ricky! I've been a fool!"

He caught her in his arms then and nearly crushed the breath from her. His mouth locked on hers in a kiss so unlike Lord Beverley's that she felt she'd swoon with delight.

"Rosie, I love you," he breathed into her ear.

She wriggled her hands and arms free so she could throw them around his neck. With something between a sob and a laugh, she declared, "I love you too. I do! But are you certain you want to marry me?"

"I'm devilish sure I cannot live without you, Rosemary Addison." A look of amusement crept into his eyes. "Let us be married soon, Rosie."

"If you wish it, Ricky," she said demurely.

Broderick grinned down at her. "So conformable! I see you're going to be a very good wife."

"And may we go to Australia and take Uncle Gordon with us to look for orchids?"

"Yes, if you really care to go, dearest." He regarded her tenderly. "As Gordon would say, you're pluck to the backbone, my gel!"

"Not really," she said, grinning wickedly. "I just want you to discover a new flower and name it after my glove!"